The Truth About Riley

Sinéad MORIARTY

The Truth About Riley

Gill Books

Gill Books
Hume Avenue
Park West
Dublin 12
www.gillbooks.ie

Gill Books is an imprint of M.H. Gill and Co.

978 07171 9521 3

Design and print origination by O'K Graphic Design, Dublin
Printed by CPI Group (UK) Ltd, Croydon, CR0 4YY
This book is typeset in 12/17 pt Adobe Garamond.

The paper used in this book comes from the wood pulp of sustainably managed forests.

A CIP catalogue record for this book is available from the British Library.

5 4 3 2 1

To my three children, the lights of my life.

'A person is a person,
whether they live in a house or a box'

— ANONYMOUS

CHAPTER 1

Riley sat in her bedroom, chewing her nails. She had started biting them recently and, even though she knew she shouldn't, she couldn't stop. She tried to only bite her thumbnails, but sometimes she moved on to her other fingers.

Downstairs, she could hear her mum's voice getting louder. She never used to listen to her mum's conversations, but now she listened to everything.

Riley opened her bedroom door and stuck her head out so she could hear what was being said.

'What do you mean, this week? I have nowhere to go! You *can't* kick us out. I haven't been able to find a job yet. I've got a twelve-year-old daughter to look after!'

Mum had been surprised when the estate agent, Mr Geoghan, had asked for a meeting earlier in the week. Now Riley couldn't believe what she was hearing. He sounded sad but firm. 'Alison, I'm sorry, but I've given you three months' leeway, on top of the notice period. The new owners have decided to move back to Ireland early. They own the property now. There's nothing I can do. It's their house.'

'Call them, tell them to wait until I get sorted. I need more time!' Mum's voice sounded panicky. Riley gripped the handle of her bedroom door tighter.

'Alison, they're moving back from America, they have three kids, they own the house and they arrive on Friday. You have to leave on Wednesday so the contract cleaners can come in on Thursday.'

Mum continued to plead and beg, but Mr Geoghan wouldn't change his mind. At last, Riley heard the front door close and Mum collapse onto the floor, crying.

Mum never used to cry, but she cried a lot these days. First, she'd cried when Dad had died. Then, when she found out about the big mess he'd left behind, she'd cried even harder. Now, it seemed like she never stopped crying.

Riley didn't cry at all any more. She'd cried when she found out her dad had died, obviously. She'd cried buckets and buckets every day for weeks. But she'd found that crying didn't help. People said it made you feel better, that it 'got out all the sadness', but it didn't work for her. Blocking things out did. So now, when sad thoughts entered Riley's head, she just ignored them.

You had to be strong in life. That's what Dad used to say. He said, 'I came from nothing. I grew up poor, but I was strong and I worked hard. And look at us now. Look at our big house and our flash cars. This is the life I dreamt of – the good life, the rich life – and it's all for you. The life of Riley, indeed!'

Dad had grown up in an orphanage with his brother, Martin. He'd left school at fourteen and started working on the street markets in the city centre. When mobile phones first came to Ireland, Dad had realised that they were going to be huge. So he'd started selling them. By the time he was eighteen, he'd opened his first mobile phone shop. He kept opening more and more until he had forty shops all over the country.

He used to go on TV and radio and tell his story – how he went from rags to riches. He told people that they could be rich too, if they were smart and took risks. Dad was all about taking risks.

Sometimes Mum would ask him to stop taking so many. But Dad would just laugh it off.

The two of them had been so different. Dad was loud and excitable, always coming up with new business ideas and working too hard. Mum was gentle and calm, preferring to stay home, looking after Riley, making their home beautiful and cosy, treating her to days out and trips to the nail salon. Riley loved hanging out with Mum; they always had fun together.

But after Dad died, they found out that he had taken far too many risks. He'd opened too many shops too quickly, and his luck had run out. Now they had no money. When Mum spoke to the bank they'd told her that Dad had emptied all their bank accounts trying to save his business. But it hadn't worked: he had lost everything, and he hadn't paid the rent on their house for the last four months. The bank manager also told Mum that Dad hadn't paid off her credit card bill.

Mum couldn't understand it. She kept saying, 'How could this happen? How could he not tell me? How did I miss this?' Then she'd cry and say, 'I'm so stupid, I'm pathetic.'

Riley felt sick when Mum wept and said she was stupid, because she wasn't. She was smart and kind and funny, and all Riley's friends adored her. She was also an amazing baker, always making muffins and fairy cakes and chocolate chip cookies for when her friends came round. She was the best mum ever.

Well ... she used to bake all those things. In the months since Dad had died, Mum hadn't done any baking. Instead, she spent all her time looking through Dad's papers, or on the phone saying, 'I don't understand, how can it all be gone?' Or she'd be out selling the jewellery Dad had given her so that they had enough money to buy food and petrol and pay some bills. She also spent a lot of time looking for a job, but so far she hadn't had any luck.

But mostly, now, Mum just cried. A lot. She tried to hide it from Riley, but Riley could see it in her puffy red eyes each morning.

Riley stood at her bedroom door, listening to her mother sobbing downstairs, and wished for the millionth time that they could go back to when their life was happy and normal.

What was going to happen to them now?

They were about to lose their home.

CHAPTER 2

A t dinner that night, Mum pushed her pasta around her plate. They had pasta almost every night now because it was cheap and it filled you up. But Mum hardly ate any of it. She had got really skinny since Dad had died; she never seemed hungry.

Riley crossed her fingers under the table. 'How did the interview go today? Do you think it went well? Do you think you might get the job?'

Mum put her fork down and rubbed her eyes. 'No, love, I won't get it because I have no experience at anything. You know what, Riley? I was an idiot. I should never have dropped out of college when I met your dad. I should have stayed and finished my law degree and got a proper job. I got swept up by him and we married too young and I never qualified at anything. I became a mum, and your dad said he didn't want me to work, and I stupidly agreed. And now he's gone, and I can't get a job because I'm not qualified for, or good at, *anything*.'

'But you *are* good at things, Mum,' Riley said.

'Like what?'

'Like, baking and … and doing nails and organising amazing birthday parties and making the house beautiful … and all that.' Riley trailed off, wishing she could think of more things her mum was good at, but her brain was all muddled up since Dad had died.

It had all happened so suddenly. Dad had gone to work as usual, and then, just after morning break, Riley had been called to the headmistress's office. She'd been terrified that Mrs Hamlin had found out that she'd left assembly early with Sophie, snuck in to the room where the cake sale was taking place and eaten a full plate of brownies. She'd been ready for a huge telling-off, but it had been so much worse than that. Nothing could have prepared Riley for opening the headmistress's door and seeing Mum sitting in a chair, tears streaming down her face.

A heart attack, the doctor had said, probably stress-related. Dad had been found slumped over his desk in the office.

'We're on our own,' Mum had sobbed, and whatever anyone said, there was no comforting her.

Riley didn't really know any of her other relations. On her dad's side there was only Uncle Martin, who was in and out of rehab with drink and drug addictions. He wasn't able to help himself, let alone them. And she had never even met her mum's parents because they had had a big fight with Mum when she'd dropped out of college and run off to marry Dad. They'd begged her to finish her law degree, but Mum had ignored them. Mum's parents were so upset with her that they never spoke to her again.

They lived somewhere in Galway, but Mum never talked about them. When Riley had asked her dad about it, he'd just said that Mum was very sad and angry that her parents were so cruel and that it was best never to mention it.

Riley thought they must be awful people to just banish Mum from their lives. She could never imagine her own mum ignoring her, whatever happened. It was a horrible thing to do. She knew her mum was sad about it, though, because she'd found her once looking at photos from when she was young. Riley had asked to see them, but Mum had closed the box and said, 'That's all in the past now. My parents have made it clear that they don't want to see me, so I have to forget them. I can promise you one thing though, Riley: no matter what decisions you make – even if they are bad ones – I will never, ever abandon you.'

She'd held Riley tight and kissed her a million times. Riley had felt so safe and loved.

Now Mum smiled at her across the table. 'You are so sweet, Riley, but I don't think baking and home-making are going to get me a job. I'm qualified for nothing.'

Riley reached out and squeezed her hand. 'It'll be OK, Mum.'

Mum picked her hand up and kissed it. 'What would I do without you? My wonderful Riley.'

'What did Mr Geoghan say earlier?' Riley asked. Even though she knew the answer, she was hoping that maybe he'd changed his mind.

Mum's face clouded over. 'We have to move out on

Wednesday. But don't worry. I'll figure something out.'

Wednesday was four days away! How was Mum going to figure it out by then? They had no money and she had no job.

Riley's head began to throb. Where were they going to go? Would she have to leave school? She knew the fees were high. But she loved school, and she didn't want to leave. But she should offer – if she was a good person she'd offer.

'Mum, I can leave Saint Mary's and go to a school with no fees.'

Mum's eyes watered. 'No, Riley, the school fees were paid in full in September. It's the one good thing your dad did before … before he lost everything and … well …' Mum coughed to hide the fact that she was about to cry. 'It's your final year in primary school and I want you to enjoy this last term as much as you can. Your education is my priority. You are not going to make the same stupid mistakes I did. You'll go to college and get a proper degree so you can support yourself in the future.'

Riley breathed out. She was so relieved. School was the one place where she could escape from all the bad stuff that was going on.

CHAPTER 3

Sophie waved her arms around excitedly as she described her upcoming party.

'It's going to be off the charts. My mum has gone really nuts this year. She's actually turning the house into a full-on spa. We're going to get manicures, pedicures, facials, boho blow-dries *and* get our make-up done! And then, she's hired this whole, like, disco party bus to drive us around and we can dance inside it and then head back to our house for a big sleepover with tons of treats and presents for everyone. We bought five fab sets of silk pyjamas yesterday – a different colour for everyone. Yours is the best, obviously.' Sophie linked her arm through Riley's.

'What colour?'

'Turquoise.'

Riley smiled. 'My favourite.'

'Duh, like, we've been besties for five years, I know what you like.'

Riley leaned in to her friend. 'Thanks, Soph.'

'And we've made up party bags for everyone with face masks and foot creams and sparkly nail varnishes and lip glosses and candles and other surprises.'

Riley couldn't wait. It sounded fantastic. Sophie's parties were always amazing. Riley reckoned Sophie's mum went overboard because Sophie was the youngest of five kids and the only girl. Sophie said that her mum, Trisha, was so happy when she was born, finally a girl after four boys, that she bought everyone in the whole maternity hospital a bottle of champagne!

Vanessa, Sophie's cousin, came over, ruining their little moment. 'Hey, Sophie, less than two weeks to go to the party!' she said.

'I know, I am literally counting the seconds,' Sophie replied.

'My mum said we had to buy you an extra-special present because it's your last birthday in primary

13

school. You are going to be *super* happy when you see what we bought you!'

While Sophie's eyes lit up, Riley's heart sank. She had no money to buy Sophie any present, never mind a good one. In the old days, Riley and her mum would go shopping and spend ages buying the perfect present for each of the parties Riley was invited to. But now … well, now there was barely enough money for food, and they had to find a new place to live because in 48 hours they were going to be kicked out of their home.

'Ooooh, I'm excited!' Sophie's eyes shone.

'Have you got your present for Sophie yet?' Vanessa asked Riley.

'Uhm, no, not yet.'

Sophie squeezed her arm. 'You don't have to buy me anything, Riley. You've got enough going on.'

'She's supposed to be your best friend. Best friends always buy each other presents,' Vanessa said.

Sophie glared at her cousin. 'She's had a horrible time with her dad and all. It's the last thing she needs to think about.'

'I know, but he died, like, months ago.'

'OMG, Vanessa, he was her *dad*,' Sophie hissed.

'It's fine. Of course I'm buying Sophie a present.' Riley wanted to kick Vanessa really hard right in the shin. As if four months was enough time to 'get over' your beloved dad dropping dead. Thankfully, no one knew about his business collapsing. Mum had told people that she'd sold it because she didn't know how to run it. No one else knew how bad things were. Mum had said not to tell anyone. She was worried that people would pity them and she didn't want pity. She was too ashamed to ask anyone for help.

Riley didn't want anyone to know that they were poor now, either. She didn't want anyone to know that they had eaten pasta and butter for the last three weeks, every single night. She didn't want anyone to know that she would have no home in two days, *especially* not Vanessa.

Vanessa had always been jealous of Sophie and Riley's closeness. When she'd moved home from London and arrived in their class last September, it had been really weird. She kept trying to own Sophie because they were cousins, and she had this annoying fake English accent.

Sophie said that she had to be nice to Vanessa because she was her cousin, and family was important. She also said that Vanessa was quite nice 'underneath it all'.

Riley had looked hard, but had concluded that –

underneath, over and sideways – Vanessa was a big pain in the bum.

At lunch time in the dining hall, Sophie pulled out her Thermos. The smell was amazing. Chicken fried rice, Riley's favourite.

'Ohhhh, not poxy rice again. I told Mum I wanted lasagne today,' Sophie complained.

Vanessa was chomping down her roast chicken and chorizo bagel. Riley's stomach rumbled. She had no lunch today because Mum had been too busy on the computer this morning, trying to find them a home, to make it – and anyway, the only bread they had in the house was out of date and had gone mouldy. Riley hadn't had breakfast, either, because there was no milk. So today she had eaten exactly one handful of dry cornflakes.

'Where's your lunch?' Sophie suddenly noticed Riley wasn't eating.

'I had a huge breakfast so I'm skipping lunch,' Riley lied.

'OMG, are you on a diet?' Vanessa asked, as crumbs spat out of her full mouth.

'No, I just had a big breakfast and was in a rush so

I knew I'd be fine,' Riley lied, and hoped her stomach wouldn't gurgle again.

'Will you please have some of my rice? I can only face half of it.' Sophie pushed the Thermos towards her friend and handed her a fork.

'Are you sure?'

'Yes.'

'OK, maybe just a bit of it.' Riley tried not to wolf the food down and chewed every bit slowly, savouring the gorgeous flavours.

Vanessa's beady eyes were watching her. 'For someone who wasn't hungry, you certainly seem to be enjoying Sophie's lunch.'

Riley felt her face redden. She put the fork down. There was still some left and she really, really wanted it, but she didn't want Vanessa to guess anything was up.

'She's doing me a favour, Van. Mum goes mad if I don't eat all my lunch. Apparently, a good lunch will help me concentrate better in the afternoons and I'll do better in my exams. Like chicken fried rice is going to make me good at maths!' Sophie rolled her eyes.

Riley laughed. Sophie was the best: kind and funny.

If only she wasn't related to Vanessa.

CHAPTER 4

M um was waiting in the car at pick-up time, parked a little back from the school. Riley ran over to her, her heart in her mouth. *Please God, please let Mum have found a house*, Riley whispered to herself.

She knew as soon as she saw her mum's face that things were not good. Riley could see suitcases and plastic bags piled high in the big boot.

As she approached the car, Riley saw Vanessa's mother, Tanya, come over and tap on her mum's window. Riley watched her mum reluctantly roll it down.

'Hi, Alison, how are things?' Tanya asked.

'Fine, thanks.'

'Are you going on a trip? What's with all the suitcases?'

'Oh …' Mum fake laughed. 'No, we're just moving house.'

'Oh, where are you moving to?'

Mum hesitated. 'Just a few miles from where we were, not too far.'

'What's the name of the road?' Tanya was not letting it go. She was as nosy and annoying as her stupid daughter, thought Riley.

She knew her mum needed saving, so she took a deep breath and bounded over. 'Hi, Mum, you're not going to believe what happened today! Oh, hi, Tanya.'

'Hi, Riley,' said Tanya. 'I hear you're moving house.'

'Yes, it's super-exciting. Oh, I think I see Vanessa waving at you,' Riley lied.

Tanya pulled back from the car window and Riley jumped into the front seat. Mum put her foot on the accelerator and sped off before Tanya could ask any more questions or realise that her daughter was not waving at her.

'Stupid woman.' Mum's teeth were gritted.

'Yeah, Vanessa's just the same, so nosy.' Riley waited a beat and then asked, 'So, where are we going? *Did* you find a place?'

Mum's hands gripped the steering wheel tightly. Looking straight ahead she said, 'Not exactly. I haven't been able to get anywhere because I don't have enough money for a deposit and the first month's rent. But the good news is I finally found a job.'

Riley tried to focus on the good news. 'Great, where?'

Her mum coughed. 'Well, it's in a restaurant in town –'

'And you'll make all their cakes?'

'Not exactly … It's a Polish restaurant. I'll be helping in the kitchen, tidying and cleaning up and that kind of thing.'

Cleaning up? Was her mum going to be washing up in a restaurant?

'Oh,' was all Riley could think of to say.

'It's a good, solid job, Riley,' her mother said. 'It doesn't pay very much, but my boss is going to let me do overtime for the first few weeks so that I can get enough money for us to rent a place.'

'But where are we going to live now?' Riley asked.

'Well, I'm not sure. I thought maybe we could ask Trisha and Sophie if we could stay there for a few days?'

No way. Riley didn't want Sophie to know she had no house. She'd tell Vanessa and then everyone would know. She didn't want the whole school finding out how bad things were.

'No, Mum, please, not Sophie. What about Uncle Martin?' she begged.

'He's in rehab again.'

'What about your friends from Pilates or … or …' Riley suddenly realised that her mum didn't have many friends. There were the women she did Pilates with twice a week, and she would go to coffee mornings with Riley's friends' mums sometimes, and there was Una from down the road, but that was kind of it.

Come to think of it, Mum and Dad hadn't really had many friends together either. Dad was always busy working and Mum really just focused on him and Riley.

'I can't ask any of those Pilates women. I only know them in a chit-chat kind of way. And I can't ask Una because I found out that your dad borrowed money from her husband and never paid it back.'

Riley could feel herself beginning to panic. Where were they going to stay? She tried to think of other women she'd heard her mum talk about …

'What about Sally, that woman you went to school with from Galway?'

Mum's face darkened. 'I can't tell Sally. She'd tell her mother and then my family would find out what a mess my life is and that they were right about your dad after all. I won't let them throw it back in my face. I'm too ashamed, Riley.'

Riley understood how her mum felt, but where were they going to sleep?

'Well, just for tonight, we could sleep in the car, and tomorrow in work I'll ask around and see if anyone there knows someone who would let me have a place without paying money upfront. The chef or the waitress in the restaurant might know landlords who are more flexible.'

In the car? Had she actually just said that? They were going to sleep in the car? Had Mum gone mad?

'But how can we … I mean, where do we … ?'

Mum pulled over and took Riley's hand in hers. 'Sweetheart, I know this is difficult, I know this is kind of a nightmare, but I'll sort it. I'll figure something out. It'll only be for a night or two. I promise.'

Riley could see sweat beading on her mum's forehead. She looked exhausted and totally stressed.

'OK, Mum. It'll be fine, don't worry.'

'Good girl. We'll pretend it's an adventure.'

Adventures don't include dead fathers, no money and sleeping in your car, Riley thought, but she said nothing.

They had only a little money left from Mum selling her jewellery, and they had to make it last until she got paid in one week's time. So they went to the supermarket and bought bread, cheese, water and butter. Riley couldn't face another week of cheese sandwiches, but she said nothing. It was the cheapest thing and it lasted longer than meat.

They had no cooker or fridge or microwave. Mum had packed some bowls and plates and cutlery but she could only fit a few things in the car. The big boot was packed with suitcases full of clothes and books, wedged in with blankets and duvets and pillows, with Riley's striped cuddly toy cat, Tiger, sitting on top.

Riley had had Tiger since she was four years old. He was her favourite cuddly animal and the one she slept with every night. She didn't want her friends to know, though, as it was a bit babyish, so she hid him whenever they came over to the house. But each night, she pulled Tiger out and held him tight. She was glad Mum had put him in.

'I've been thinking about where the best place to park is,' said Mum. 'We don't want anyone to see us but we want to be safe, so I googled it. Apparently, supermarket car parks are the safest. So I thought we'd park here, around the back. Isn't that hilarious? You can google where to sleep in your car.' Mum's voice had gone really high and squeaky and her eyes were all shiny and weird. She looked as if she was fighting back tears.

Riley nodded and said it sounded good. But she was terrified. What if someone broke into their car and attacked or robbed them, or kidnapped her? Maybe she *should* ask Trisha and Sophie if they could stay with them. But then she thought about Vanessa finding out and shivered. Sophie couldn't lie, so if Vanessa asked her why Riley was staying, Sophie would say it was because she had no house, and Vanessa would know that Riley's mum had only pretended they had a new home. It would all be a huge mess and so embarrassing.

It was better just to sleep in the car and hope that the people Mum was working for would know someone who could rent them a house.

They parked the car around the back of the supermarket car park at dusk. They got out, then went into the public toilet and brushed their teeth and went to the loo. It stank and there was wee all over the floor. Riley tried not to step in it. It was horrible. She thought about her lovely bathroom at home, with its fluffy towels and gorgeous shower gel, and tried not to cry. She had to be strong for Mum.

Back at the car, they moved all of their suitcases and bags into the back seat so they could make a sleeping area in the long boot. If they both lay diagonally, they would be able to fit. It would be a bit of a squash, but at least they could stretch out their legs.

They stuck black bin bags over the windows and the back of the boot with Sellotape, so they could have some privacy. Then, Mum pulled out a plastic bag and handed Riley her pyjamas. They both had to wriggle out of their clothes and into their night things in the boot. It was really hard and they were sweating by the time they had finished.

Mum laid two big duvets in the boot to give them something soft to lie on and then put two more big duvets over the top. She pulled two pillows out for their heads and then clambered under the covers. Riley snuggled up beside her.

Mum put her arms around Riley. 'I'm so sorry about this, love. I'm a rubbish mum, but I'll make it better. I promise you, I will make this better.'

Riley held her mum close. 'You're not rubbish, and I love you, Mum.'

'I love you so much, Riley. You are my world,' Mum whispered back.

Riley squeezed her eyes shut so she wouldn't cry. She held Tiger up to her chin and felt his soft fur against her skin. The comfort of him helped her to drift into a fitful sleep.

CHAPTER 5

Riley woke up stiff. The duvets had helped a little bit, but the cold, hard surface of the boot was still difficult to sleep on. Riley missed her lovely bed. In her house, she'd had a big double bed with the softest mattress and mattress cover. It had been like sleeping on a cloud. Now, she felt as if she had slept on concrete.

Her bed at home had had a canopy over it, covered in twinkly lights. When Riley was in bed, it was like being in a magical tent with stars shining above her. She'd loved that bed. It had been her tenth birthday present from Mum and Dad – along with lots of other gifts. But it was her favourite present. She'd lie there with Tiger, looking up at the 'stars', imagining she was a princess.

Riley quietly turned her head. Mum was awake, staring at her phone. Riley peered over and saw that Mum was scrolling through family photos. Photos of her, Dad and Mum on holiday in Italy last year. Riley felt her chest tighten; she couldn't think about Dad now. She couldn't think about happy times or how amazing her life used to be. It hurt too much. She had to focus on now, on today. If she let herself think about the past, she'd just get upset. And what was the point, anyway? The past was over – she had to deal with the present, with now, today, this morning. And right now, Riley had to get up and go to school before anyone saw her.

She yawned and stretched her arms so her mum would know she was awake.

Alison snapped her phone off and turned to Riley. 'Morning, sunshine.'

'Morning.'

'Did you sleep OK?' Mum asked.

'Yes, really well,' Riley lied. She'd woken up about twenty times. She kept hearing noises, unsure whether they were in her head, her dreams or real. Either way, she had slept really badly and she was now stiff, hungry and tired.

'Me too,' Mum said, but Riley knew she was lying too. Her hair was sticking up in all directions, her face was pale, and she looked exhausted. Mum pulled on a pair of jeans and a sweatshirt. Riley was used to seeing her mum perfectly dressed and made up, with blow-dried hair and immaculate, polished nails. She loved that her mum was so glamorous; it made her proud. But now Mum looked tired and old.

'Come on, sleepyhead.' Mum nudged her. 'Get your uniform on.'

Riley wriggled out of her pyjamas and into her uniform. She kept hitting her mum in the face with her arms when she was putting on her shirt, so Mum stepped out of the car.

When Riley was dressed, they went back to the smelly bathroom to brush their teeth. It was locked.

'Dammit,' Mum said. 'They must lock it at night.'

Riley looked at her watch. It was only seven. 'If you drop me at school, we can sneak in and use the bathroom there. No one will be in this early.'

Mum smiled. 'Good idea.'

They drove into the school yard. There was only one car in the car park; it belonged to the school caretaker. The main door was locked but Riley could see the caretaker through the glass, polishing the floor. She knocked and waved.

He came over to the door.

'Sorry,' said Riley, 'I just need to get in early to … to … get some books that I forgot. I need to finish a project that has to be in and, uh … well, could you let us in, please?'

He took out a big bunch of keys and unlocked the door.

'Thank you,' Riley said.

'Thanks so much.' Mum put out her hand. 'I'm Riley's mum, Alison.'

'Nice to meet you. I'm Oleg.' The caretaker glanced down at the towel and toothpaste sticking out of Mum's bag.

'Come on, Mum.' Riley tugged at her mum's sleeve, and they rushed towards the bathroom.

In case anyone else came to school early, Mum blocked the main bathroom door so Riley could go to the toilet, then wash her face and brush her teeth. Then Riley did the same for her mum. When they were finished, they felt fresher and better.

They went back to the car and Mum handed Riley two cheese sandwiches – made with dry bread with hunks of cheese in the middle. 'Sorry, love, I couldn't butter the bread. The butter's rock hard from the cold. This will have to keep you going until I pick you up.'

'It's fine,' Riley lied.

'It's not fine at all.' Mum looked upset.

Riley hugged her mother. 'It's OK, Mum, it's just for a few days.'

She gave Riley a sad smile back. 'Thanks, pet. I have to go now or I'll be late. I can't pick you up until five, so you'll have to go the library and do your homework there, OK?'

'Sure, no problem.' Riley didn't mind that. Trying to do her homework in the car last night had been really difficult. At least the library had desks and heating and a clean toilet she could use.

They hugged and Riley waved as her mother drove off. She turned to go back into school and saw Oleg watching her.

She looked down and scurried past him, holding her dry sandwiches in one hand and her school backpack in the other.

Riley was starving. She sat in the empty classroom and tried to eat some of the dry bread, washed down with water from her water bottle. It made her want to gag, but she forced herself. She knew she needed food to get her through the long day ahead.

Before long, the school began to fill up with teachers and girls. Riley's head throbbed and her eyes stung from lack of sleep. She plastered a smile on her face and tried to chat to her friends as if everything was normal, as if she hadn't just spent the night in the boot of her car.

At break-time, they all ran out to the yard. Some of the girls went to hang out on the hockey pitches, some on the tennis courts. Riley, Sophie and Vanessa headed to their usual spot under the big oak tree.

Sophie and Vanessa were carrying their break snacks. Sophie had a muffin and Vanessa had a flapjack.

The smell of the flapjack made Riley's stomach groan. Her mum used to make the best flapjacks, chewy and delicious, as well as muffins and scones and buns and cakes and … She pinched her leg to distract herself from the memories.

'Urgh, this flapjack is gross. Mum always burns the edges,' complained Vanessa. 'She's the worst cook.' She wrapped it up and tossed it in the bin beside them.

Sophie gobbled up her muffin as they talked about her party the following Friday.

'Mum's ordered a chocolate fountain!' said Sophie, grinning.

Riley closed her eyes. In one week and one day she would be stuffing her face with chocolate-covered marshmallows and strawberries and pineapple and … oh God, it would be the best night ever. Grace and Zoe were coming to the party too. Riley liked them both and they'd stop Vanessa from taking over.

'Your mum is so great,' Riley said.

'Yeah, she's my favourite aunt by miles. And I'm her favourite niece,' Vanessa interjected, always ready to remind Riley that she was related to Sophie. 'I'll come over early to help you set up, Soph.'

'Actually, Riley already offered,' Sophie said.

'Fine, whatever, I was just trying to be nice,' Vanessa snapped.

'Of course, if you want to come over then too, that's fine,' Sophie said, trying to smooth things over.

Please say no, thought Riley, crossing her fingers. She wanted to get ready with Sophie on her own and help her set up and maybe get to eat some of the treats early.

Vanessa flicked back her long honey-coloured hair. 'No, it's fine, I'll just spend longer getting ready. I've got four new outfits and I don't know which one I'm going to wear, so I'll be busy trying all my new clothes on.'

The bell rang and they stood up to go in. Sophie rolled her eyes at Riley, who tried not to laugh. She was delighted Vanessa wasn't coming over early to help set up the party. Vanessa had the amazing ability to ruin everything by complaining or making it all about her.

As they walked back towards school, Riley said, 'I think I dropped my pen. Go ahead, I'll follow you in.'

She rushed back to the tree, looked around to make sure no one was watching, and then fished Vanessa's flapjack out of the bin. She ate it in three big bites. It tasted amazing, buttery and oaty and delicious. Even the burnt edges tasted good. How could Vanessa have not liked it?

When Riley turned to go back in, she saw the caretaker fixing one of the tennis nets. Had he seen her? She prayed he hadn't. She didn't want anyone to know she was eating food out of a bin.

Riley rushed back into class. Her legs weren't shaking with hunger any more and she didn't feel so light-headed. With some more bread and cheese for lunch she'd make it through the day.

CHAPTER 6

Riley sat in the boot of the car, barely pausing to chew as she shoved the food Mum had brought back from the restaurant into her mouth. It was a Polish dish called *bigos*. It had cabbage in it, which Riley normally hated, but she was so hungry that she didn't care, and anyway it had sausage and onions and other stuff too. It was delicious.

'Slow down,' Mum said. 'You'll get indigestion.'

But Riley couldn't. All she'd had today was a flapjack and some dry bread and cheese.

'How was work?' Riley asked, when she finally stopped chewing. Her stomach felt as if it was about to burst. She closed the top of the now-empty Tupperware box and put it beside her.

'Work was fine.' Mum looked out the window.

'Did you ask them if they knew anyone with a house or apartment to rent?'

Mum nodded. 'Yes, they said they'd ask around.'

'OK, good.' Riley lay back on the pile of duvets and pillows. Her mum lay down beside her. She smelled of fried food and cleaning products. Her sweatshirt was stained and dirty, and her hair was greasy and pulled back into a ponytail. She didn't look like Mum at all.

'I have a French project to do this weekend so I'm going back to Sophie's after school tomorrow,' Riley said. Going to Sophie's to work on a project together was perfectly normal, so it wouldn't seem weird to anyone that she was there, and hopefully she'd be able to have some food there too. 'So, I won't have to stay in the car while you're working late,' she added.

But Mum wasn't listening. She was already fast asleep, her mouth wide open. Her hands had fallen by her sides and Riley noticed how red and raw they were.

She gently pulled a duvet up to cover them both and snuggled in beside her mum. She was exhausted too. It had been a very long twenty-four hours.

Boom! Boom!

Riley bolted upright. It was still dark. 'Mum!' she squealed.

Mum sat up beside her, eyes wide with fear.

'I know you're in there!' a man's voice shouted.

They saw a pair of eyes looking in at them through a gap in the black plastic bags they had put over the windows earlier.

Riley's heart was pounding.

'Go away!' Mum shouted.

'Do you have any food?' another man's voice asked.

'No.'

'I want food.'

The car began to shake.

Oh my God, they're rocking the car! They're going to push it over! Riley began to cry. 'Mum, what are we going to do?'

'Hang on, love,' Mum whispered, as she climbed over the back seat and into the front of the car.

She put the key in the ignition and started the engine. Slamming her foot on the accelerator, Mum jerked the car forward. They bolted out of the car park at high speed and didn't stop until they were a few miles away.

Mum pulled over and rested her head on the steering wheel, breathing heavily. Riley's whole body was shaking. She could hear her mum muttering. 'I can't take this. I hate you, Frank, how could you do this to us? You useless –!' Her mum swore and began to cry.

Riley slid over the back seat and hugged her from behind. They sat crying for all that they had lost – a husband, a father, a home, safety, security, a place to live …

It was still dark outside. Riley looked at her watch. It was five in the morning but she didn't feel tired; her heart was still pounding from the fright.

Mum's breathing steadied. She pulled her head back up and wiped away her tears.

'OK, we need a safer place to park. I'll figure something out. For now, let's go to the twenty-four-hour Starbucks and sit in a warm café. I have enough money for one hot chocolate – we can share.'

Riley nodded. She was afraid to speak. She felt so many emotions rising up in her chest – worry, fear, grief, anxiety … She couldn't stop shaking.

Her mum drove to the Starbucks in town and they found a parking space outside. They climbed out, Riley in her pyjama bottoms, Mum in the clothes she'd fallen asleep in. They pulled hoodies on and slipped their bare feet into runners. The café was empty except for one couple in the corner, a young guy on his laptop and two staff members behind the counter.

Mum ordered one hot chocolate and counted out the change to pay for it. Riley stared at the chocolate chip muffins on display. She wanted to break the glass and grab one, just to feel the sugar inside her stomach.

Mum put her arm around Riley. 'Sorry, darling, no money for muffins. We can only pay for one hot chocolate,' she said loudly.

Riley was mortified. Why was Mum announcing to the whole café that they were broke?

The young guy serving them looked at them. 'You know, we have muffins from yesterday that we have to throw out. If you want, I can give them to you?'

'Oh no, it's fine, thank you,' Riley said hurriedly. She didn't want him to think they were trying to get free food.

'Honestly, you'd be doing me a favour by eating them. They're just going to get dumped in the bin otherwise.'

'Really?' Riley's eyes shone.

'Sure, yeah.'

'We'd love them, then, thank you,' Mum said.

The man went out to the back room and came back with three muffins. Two blueberry and one chocolate.

'Wow!' Riley took the plate.

'Thank you so much,' Mum said. 'You're very kind.'

They sat in the corner of the café, on a big squishy couch, and slowly sipped the hot chocolate and ate the muffins. Well, Riley drank most of the hot chocolate and ate two of the muffins. Mum said she wasn't very hungry. Mum charged their phones as they ate.

Riley began to feel her tense muscles relax. 'Although this has been a horrible night, it's ended up being a good one,' she said, chewing the last mouthful of chocolate muffin.

'There are good people in the world, Riley, don't forget that. And those men were probably good men too – they were just hungry and tired, like us. It's amazing how one kind gesture can make such a huge difference to someone – in this case us. We must remember that. It's so important to be kind in life.'

Mum was right; the awful night had ended well because of the nice staff member. Riley laid her head on her mum's shoulder and fell asleep in the warmth of the café.

Chapter 7

Riley fell asleep in class twice the next day. Sophie kept having to nudge her awake so Miss Caroline didn't catch her.

'What's going on with you? Were you up all night on your phone?' Sophie asked.

'Yeah, I was on Instagram for hours,' Riley said. *Oh, Sophie, if only you knew what my night was like,* she thought.

'I thought your mum was strict about taking your phone at night?'

'She is, but she forgot last night.'

'Lucky you! I was made to go to bed at nine because Tim, Tom, Fred and Ted broke two kitchen chairs. Mum and Dad were fuming and sent us all to our rooms.'

Sophie had four elder brothers, two of whom were twins. Riley knew they drove her up the wall. 'How did they break them?' she asked.

'So, Tim saw this wrestling thing on YouTube where one person sits in a kitchen chair on top of the table and the other person stands on the edge of the table and they dive on top of you. Obviously when Tim dove on top of Tom, they both fell off the table and the chair smashed. But then the twins wanted to try it because it looked like "fun" and they smashed the second chair. Ted sprained his wrist, and Fred might have a concussion, but Dad says he's a stupid fool anyway and the concussion will make no difference.'

Riley giggled. Sophie's brothers were wild. They were always in trouble. Tim was fifteen, Tom was fourteen and Fred and Ted, the twins, were thirteen.

'Dad said he'd had enough of them and was going to send them to boarding school. But then Mum started crying and said she'd miss them too much. I wish they *would* go to boarding school – the house would be so nice and quiet and not trashed all the time.'

Riley thought Sophie was so lucky to have siblings. Even if they were a pain. She hated being an only child. She wished she had a sister or brother to talk to. Especially now, when everything was so upside down.

'Anyway, don't worry about today. We can hide in my room and do our project there. Hopefully they won't come near us. It's a pity your new house is being painted – I'd love to have seen it.'

'Yeah, I know. There are painters everywhere, so it just wouldn't work,' Riley lied. She was getting good at lying.

Riley was so looking forward to going to Sophie's house after school. She knew that she'd get snacks and drinks and it would be warm and cosy and lovely. Mum had to work until ten that night, so she said she'd pick her up then. Riley had told her to park down the street and text her. She didn't want Sophie or Trisha to see the car full of bags and duvets and start asking awkward questions.

Trisha picked them up from school and handed them each a big chocolate chip cookie from Marks and Spencer. They were Riley's favourite, the best ones ever.

She wolfed hers down; she hadn't eaten since Starbucks at five o'clock that morning. Both she and

Mum had fallen asleep there and only woken at eight. The staff had left them to sleep, which was kind. She'd had to quickly get changed and washed in the Starbucks toilet and rush to school, so there'd been no time for breakfast, and Riley had forgotten to take some bread and cheese for lunch.

'It's good to see you, Riley. How's your Mum?' Trisha asked.

'She's good, thanks.'

'I've tried calling her a few times but she must be really busy.'

'Yeah, she has a new job, so she's super hectic.'

'Good for her. And Sophie tells me you've moved into a new house. How is that all going? I'm sure it wasn't easy leaving your old home,' Trisha said.

'Oh, it's fine. The new house is lovely.'

'Good, I'm glad for you. Is it close to school?'

'Yeah, not too far.' Riley loved Trisha, but she wished she wouldn't ask her so many questions. She knew Sophie's mum meant well and that she was just asking because she wanted to make sure Riley and her mum were OK, but all these questions were giving Riley a headache.

'What's your mum working at? Does she like it? If she ever needs help with lifts to school, tell her to call me. I'd be happy to help.'

Riley didn't want to say her mother was washing dishes. 'She, uhm, she's working for a Polish company, but I'm not sure exactly what she does.'

'I must talk to her about it. I think I need a job. The boys are driving me round the bend. They are like a bunch of wild animals.' Trisha held up her hand. 'Don't get me wrong, I love them, but they are a handful.'

Riley smiled and said nothing.

Sophie rolled her eyes. 'Oh my God, Mum, stop asking Riley so many questions – you're wrecking her head!'

'Fine, then, I won't say another word. I'm just happy for you that things are OK, Riley, pet.'

'Thanks, Trisha.'

When they got to Sophie's house, loud music was blaring out through the windows.

Trisha opened the front door and let the girls in. They were greeted by two naked boys.

'What in the name of God are you doing? Sophie has a friend over – put some clothes on!' Trisha roared.

'Tim and Tom said we were going to do an ice-bath challenge, but when me and Ted were getting changed into our trunks, they attacked us and sprayed Superglue over our bums and then pushed us together and we got stuck. They think it's hilarious, I hate them,' Fred roared, red in the face.

'Oh my actual God, I cannot take this house any more. You are disgusting animals!' Sophie screamed. 'Cover up!'

The boys put their hands over their private parts.

'It's not our fault, we can't unstick,' Ted hissed at her.

Trisha stood in the middle of the hall and shouted so loudly, Riley was surprised the windows didn't shatter. 'TIM AND TOM, GET DOWN HERE! I AM GOING TO KILL YOU THIS TIME!'

The older boys came down the stairs looking all innocent. 'What's wrong, Mum?'

'Don't you *what's wrong* me. You stuck your brothers' bottoms together and now they can't unstick.'

'We should put them up on YouTube!' Tim said, cracking up laughing.

'Yeah, like an Irish *Jackass*!' Tom giggled.

'I don't want to be stuck to Fred's bum forever,' Ted wailed.

Riley couldn't help smiling. It was nice to have something to laugh about. It had been a while.

'You two,' Trisha said, pointing at Tim and Tom, 'google "how to undo Superglue" right now and sort out this mess. And you two'– she pointed at the twins – 'cover yourselves up with a towel or something, for goodness' sake!'

The four boys shuffled off into the TV room.

Trisha and the girls headed into the kitchen.

'Muuuuuuuuum, they are so embarrassing.' Sophie was on the verge of tears.

'I am so sorry about that, Riley. I bet your house is a lovely, peaceful place. I am ashamed of my sons. Maybe you should go to your house to do the project. This place is like a zoo.'

'Oh no, we can't. It's being painted.' Riley quickly nipped that plan in the bud.

'Right, well, go on up to Sophie's bedroom and I'll keep them away from you,' Trisha said, kissing Sophie's head. 'Thank God I have one sane child.'

'But what about my birthday party, Mum? They can't be here.'

'They *live* here, Sophie. But don't worry – if I have to lock them in the TV room for the night, I will. Now, go on upstairs and I'll call you when dinner's ready.'

The two girls went upstairs to Sophie's bedroom. It looked so much bigger than Riley remembered. Her bed was covered in a beautiful patchwork blanket and she had coloured butterfly lights hanging down the wall behind her bed like a curtain. Her desk was up against one wall and on the opposite wall was a huge noticeboard with photos, postcards with positive messages, and dreamcatchers pinned on it.

They sat cross-legged, facing each other on Sophie's big bed, and worked on their project for a while. One of the questions was 'What does your father do?'

Sophie paused. 'We don't have to answer that one,' she said, chewing the end of her pen nervously.

'No, it's fine, I'll just say my father was a businessman.'

'A super-successful one,' Sophie added.

Riley didn't say anything. Her dad *had* been

successful, but he'd been really stupid too. He'd left her and Mum with nothing. She tried to push down the anger she felt.

'Are you OK, Riley? Are you still really sad about your dad? You never talk about him,' Sophie said gently.

Riley bit her lip. 'I'm fine. I do miss him, but I have my mum and she's amazing.' Riley thought that was enough information to stop Sophie asking any more questions. She did not want to talk about her dad.

'She really is. Of all the mums, yours is the nicest. She always looks amazing. And she's a great baker too. I can't wait to come to your house and eat one of her cakes again.'

Mum hadn't baked a cake in months and Riley wasn't sure if she ever would again. Besides, who could bake from the boot of a car?

Thankfully the conversation ended then, because Trisha called them for dinner.

They ran downstairs. Riley was so looking forward to a home-cooked meal at an actual table, sitting on an actual chair.

Trisha placed plates of chicken curry in front of them.

'Not this again,' Sophie grumbled. 'We've had it once already this week.'

'Stop your complaining and eat up. Aren't you lucky to have food on your plate? Some children in the world are starving.'

She's right, Riley thought. Sophie was being a moan. Then again, Riley had never thought about what it felt like to be starving before now. She'd never thought about how many children in the world were deprived of food. But now, well, now Riley knew how it actually felt to be hungry and to not know when your next meal was coming. Now, Riley appreciated every single bite of food she got. She didn't waste a second, but tucked straight into her curry. 'It's delicious, Trisha, thank you.'

'You're welcome, Riley. It's nice to have someone with manners in the house!'

The kitchen door burst open and the four boys came in. Thankfully they were all fully dressed. Riley was still trying to get the image of Fred's and Ted's bare bums and other bits out of her mind.

'Well, how did you separate them?' Trisha asked.

Tom grinned. 'We googled "how to undo Superglue", and it said that the acid in lemon juice could get rid of it. So we squeezed lemon juice over their butts and then we had to use a toothbrush to rub it in and stuff and then I pulled Fred, and Tim pulled Ted, and they split.'

'My bum is killing me,' Fred said.

'They rubbed the lemon in hard with the toothbrush even though it said to rub gently, and the lemon burnt, and I can barely sit down,' Ted complained.

A roar came from the hall. Sophie's dad, Brian, came thundering into the room, holding up a toothbrush. 'Why in the name of God is the bathroom covered in lemons and lemon juice, and which animal used my toothbrush? Look at the state of it!'

The bristles were all squashed sideways and it was covered in lemon pulp.

The two older boys cracked up laughing.

Trisha held up her hands. 'Sit down and have your dinner. We have a guest.'

'Sure, Riley is well used to the mayhem in this house.' Brian winked at Riley. Then he tapped Tim and Tom over the head with the toothbrush. 'I know it was you two messers. I just can't figure out what on earth you were doing with lemons and a toothbrush.'

'Don't ask, you're better off not knowing,' Trisha assured him.

'The boys Superglued the twins' bums together,' Sophie told her father. 'Dad, I want you to send them to boarding school. I am sick and tired of living like this.'

'Superglued their bums?' Brian threw his head back and began to whoop with laughter. It was very contagious and soon everyone, even Sophie and Riley, was roaring laughing.

When her mum texted to say that she was five minutes away and would park down the road, Riley got up from the couch in the TV room where she was watching a reality show with Sophie and went to use the bathroom. On her way to the downstairs toilet, she passed the kitchen. No one was in there. Riley went in. Her heart was pounding as she listened out for any sounds. But the coast was clear.

Even though Riley knew it was wrong, even though she knew it was kind of stealing, she popped a packet of chocolate fingers and a tube of sour cream Pringles up her jumper, and then pulled her backpack into the bathroom with her so she could hide the food inside it.

Riley knew she'd done a bad thing, but she also knew that her mum wasn't going to get paid until next Wednesday. Riley had the whole weekend stretching ahead of her and she couldn't face dry bread and cheese for breakfast, lunch *and* dinner. She needed a treat, she deserved something nice, right? And Sophie's mum probably wouldn't even notice. And if Trisha knew the situation Riley was in, she'd be happy to give her food. She knew it.

Riley zipped up her backpack and went to say goodbye and thank you to her best friend's parents. The same people she had just stolen from.

Chapter 8

Riley sat in the corner of the restaurant working on her project. Mum's Polish boss, Maja, had said Riley could use the corner table in the early mornings and in the afternoons, if it was quiet. Aleksy, the chef, and Zofia, the waitress, waved at her. They worked really hard and didn't speak much English, so Riley hadn't got to know them yet.

Maja owned the restaurant. She was nice, but also a bit scary. Her English was good, but Riley found her difficult to understand sometimes because her accent was a bit strong.

Riley was answering maths questions when Maja came over and handed her a hot chocolate.

'Thank you.' Riley sipped the lovely drink, feeling it warm up her cold body. It had been really cold in the car last night and she hadn't slept properly since those men had frightened them. Riley knew they were just hungry too, but their shouting and shaking the car had been terrifying. Riley felt exhausted. The sugar from the hot chocolate helped perk her up.

'You are living in your car, yes?' Maja asked.

'Yes.' Riley knew her mum had spoken to Maja about everything, so she didn't need to lie to her, at least.

'This is bad.'

'Uhm, well … yes, but we'll find a place soon.'

Maja snorted. 'Finding place is not so easy. Ireland is very difficult place to find a home.'

Riley's heart sank.

'Everybody says Irish people are so nice, welcoming everybody. I have met nice Irish people but also bad Irish people. Not all Irish people are welcoming. Some are making it hard for foreigners to find house or flat. Landlords are asking for big money for terrible flats. Government need to do something. Landlords are big bullies.'

Are they? Riley wondered. Oh no, if the landlords

were bullies and asking for big money, they'd *never* find a place to live. And were Irish people not welcoming? Riley had never thought about it before.

'Your mummy says you are a good girl, you do good in school. Keep working. You need to be smart, go to university and get big job.'

'I will.' Riley hesitated and then said, 'Maja, do you think Mum will find an apartment soon?'

'No. It will take weeks, but I am helping. I am asking and I am looking.'

'Oh.' Riley's heart sank. *Weeks?* She couldn't face another night in the car – how was she going to cope with weeks? She went into the restaurant bathroom and had a little cry.

Then she opened the packet of chocolate fingers she had taken from Sophie's house and ate three. She knew she should save them and only have one a day, but she was feeling sad and she wanted three, so she ate them.

The door opened and Mum came in. Seeing Riley's blotchy face, she asked, 'Are you OK?'

Riley nodded. 'I'm fine, just tired.'

'Oh, sweetie, I know. But guess what? Maja just said we can sleep in here tonight. When all the customers

58

have gone and we've cleaned up, we can get our duvets and sleep in her little office off the kitchen.'

'Really?' Riley was thrilled. This meant they'd be safe inside an actual building. No people knocking on the car windows or shaking the car or threatening to break in and rob them.

She hugged her mum. It was then that Alison noticed the chocolate fingers poking out of Riley's backpack.

'Where did you get those?' she asked.

Riley's face went bright red. 'Trisha gave them to me.'

'Riley?' Her mum's eyes were like lasers, burning the truth out of her.

'OK, I took them, but they had another full packet in the cupboard.'

Mum's hand flew up to her mouth. 'Oh my God, Riley, did you steal them?'

'It wasn't like that. If I asked, and Trisha knew that we were living in our car, she'd give me food and money and everything. But I didn't say anything – I just took that one small thing.'

'No, Riley.' Mum was firm. 'Stealing is stealing, even if it's just a packet of biscuits. It's wrong. You know that.'

Riley felt anger flare up inside her. 'I couldn't face another weekend of stale bread and cheese, Mum. I'm starving, I need some little treats. This is a nightmare. I hate my life. So stop giving me a hard time because I did one small bad thing.'

Mum put her hands on Riley's shoulders. 'Riley, if we start behaving badly, even just small wrong things, we will end up in a much worse situation. We have to be strong but also honest and true to ourselves. You are not a kid who steals. Don't start now. I know this is awful, but I promise it'll get better soon. Please don't ever take anything that is not yours again. Promise?'

Riley nodded.

'Aleeeeeeson,' Maja called from outside. 'We need you to clean now.'

Riley watched her mum straighten up and sigh before walking out the door. She looked as exhausted as Riley felt.

Sleeping in Maja's office was much better than the car. Riley and her mum could stretch out fully. Although the floor was hard and the carpet was old and bald in many places, at least it was safe. Riley slept, but kept having nightmares about everyone in school finding out she had stolen from her best friend and gathering around her, screaming nasty things in her face.

Despite the bad dreams, she woke up feeling a little bit better. It was Sunday and the restaurant was closed, which meant that she and Mum could spend the whole day here. They could make cups of tea and hot chocolate, though Mum said not to eat any of the food in the kitchen. Maja had left a few things out for them to eat: bread and butter and salami and some leftover potato pancakes and a bar of dark chocolate.

Mum said they needed to have a proper wash and they needed to clean Riley's school shirts and pants and socks from the last few days.

They took off their clothes in the toilet. Mum handed Riley a facecloth and they both washed themselves from head to toe. She was shocked at how thin her mum was; her ribs were sticking out. It felt a bit strange being naked in a bathroom with her. Riley was embarrassed at first but Mum just carried on cleaning herself, so Riley did too. They bent their heads into the sink and washed their hair under the tap using hand soap.

It was hard to believe that only a week ago Riley had been showering in her own bathroom. She'd loved that bathroom. The walls were painted turquoise, her favourite colour, and the shower tiles were white with tiny turquoise dots on them. Her shower was huge and could fit about five people. She'd had shampoo and conditioner that smelled of spring flowers and there was a hot towel rail, so when she got out she was wrapped in warm fluffiness, and the heated floor tiles were cosy under her toes. Her big sink had been crammed with all her hairbrushes and bobbins and clips and hand lotions and body creams …

Forget about it, Riley said to herself. *There's no point thinking about the past now. Focus on today and helping Mum find a new place to live. That's it.* She bent over and tried to rinse out the soap from her hair.

Riley washed her socks and pants while Mum washed Riley's school shirts and the T-shirts and sweatshirts and jeans she'd been wearing to work. They hung all the clothes up to dry on the backs of the chairs in the small restaurant and lined them up against the radiators.

Mum looked at her watch. 'OK, we have six viewings. We need to try to impress the landlord, so I'm going to dress up a bit and I need you to do the same.'

Mum pulled out a smart pair of black trousers and a baby-blue cashmere jumper from her suitcase. While her mother put make-up on, Riley pulled on black skinny jeans, a grey fluffy jumper and her black furry jacket. It was so nice to see Mum looking like herself again. Riley felt so much better for having had a wash and putting on clean clothes. Now they just needed their hair to air-dry as they walked.

The first apartment wasn't far from the restaurant. It was on a dark, narrow lane with rubbish blowing all over the road. These people were clearly not good about recycling. When they got to the address, Mum stopped and looked at the house, then checked it against the details on her phone again. Riley heard her curse quietly under her breath.

It was a small house with a basement flat. It looked old and falling down. Mum took a deep breath and rang the front doorbell. A man in a vest answered.

'Hi.' Mum smiled as brightly as possible. 'We've come about the flat to rent.'

The man looked them up and down. 'Are you serious? *You two* want to rent my basement flat?'

'Yes.' Mum kept smiling.

He shrugged, then took a key out of his pocket, and

they walked down a few steps to the basement. He opened the door and handed Mum the key.

'Lock up and give it back when you're finished.'

'Of course. Is it available immediately?' Mum asked politely.

'Yep.' He walked out.

Riley and her mum stepped inside. They looked around the dark, dank room. There was an old, sagging couch in the middle of it, a TV in the corner and a tiny kitchenette on one side, separated off by a small table and four chairs. Mould was creeping up the walls and the lino on the floor was curling up in one corner, revealing more mould underneath.

The bathroom was even worse, and the only bedroom had one full wall covered in mould.

Riley was speechless. She had no words to describe the panic rising inside her chest. Was this actually where they were going to live?

Mum kept saying things like, 'We could fix it up … a bit of paint … a lot of bleach … a few rugs …'

They walked back out, locked the door and rang the main house doorbell to hand back the keys.

'Well?' the man asked.

'It needs a bit of a clean and a paint.'

He shrugged. 'Not my problem.'

But it is his problem, Riley thought. *It's his flat. He's renting it. He owns it. Why doesn't he care how awful it is?*

'It said online the rent is eight hundred euros a month. If we painted it ourselves and did it up, could we say six hundred euros a month?' Mum gave the man her best smile.

He snorted. 'You must be joking, love. I've already had two offers, one for eight hundred and one for eight hundred and fifty. It's one month's deposit and one month's rent upfront, take it or leave it.'

Mum swallowed. 'Is there any chance I could pay you weekly and add the deposit to the rent? I don't have any money to pay you upfront.'

He shook his head. 'Nope.'

'Look, I'm desperate – I have a twelve-year-old child to look after, we're living in our car, could you please help me out?'

'I'm sorry for you, love, but I'm not running a charity here.' The man closed the door in her face.

Mum shouted a bad word at the door. Riley had never heard her mum use that word before. It was a very bad curse word.

'To hell with him,' Mum said, grabbing Riley's hand. 'It was a dump, anyway. We'll find a nicer place.'

But they didn't. Every place they saw was just as awful and some were even more expensive.

Maybe Maja was right about landlords. All the ones they had met so far were mean, greedy, nasty bullies.

CHAPTER 9

S ophie's party was in two days and Riley still had no gift for her. She was back sleeping in the car. Maja had said they could stay in her office on Saturday and Sunday nights but not during the week. She said she was very sorry and something about squatters' rights, which neither Riley nor Mum understood. Mum said they had to do whatever Maja said because she was (a) the only person who would employ her and (b) letting them stay the weekend nights there and giving them leftover food every night.

Mum was now working even longer hours to try to save up a deposit for an apartment. So every day after picking Riley up from school, she parked the car outside the restaurant until closing time. Riley stayed in the car and waited for her mum. She was allowed in to use the toilet and to brush her teeth at half-past five, before the restaurant began to fill up. After that, she could only go in if it was an emergency.

Sometimes it was midnight or even one in the morning before Mum finished work. She'd come out, and they'd drive the car around the back of the restaurant to the little car park. Riley would then help Mum lock the big gate of the car park. It was safe there. Maja had said they could park there every night after the restaurant closed.

No matter how tired she was, Riley could never sleep until her mum was snuggled up beside her. So she wasn't getting to sleep until after one o'clock most nights. Mum was usually too tired to even change into her pyjamas. She'd collapse beside Riley in her smelly work clothes and be asleep as soon as her head hit the pillow.

When Riley's alarm went off at seven, she felt terrible waking her mum up. She was always in such a deep sleep, but the restaurant didn't open until ten, so Riley had to get to school to use the bathroom there and wash and brush her teeth before anyone saw her.

Sometimes Riley worried Mum would crash the car because she was so sleepy. Mum would unlock the gate, push it open and then climb into the front seat of the car, her eyes still half-closed, and drive Riley to school. At red lights, Mum would sometimes rest her head against the steering wheel, and once she actually fell asleep. Riley had to wake her up again.

Every morning, when Mum dropped Riley off, Oleg the caretaker would see Riley arriving and would unlock the door for her.

Riley always said hello to him and smiled. He always gave her a warm hello back but never asked any questions. Riley wondered if Oleg knew why she had to come in so early. If he did, he never said, and she was grateful for that.

Today was payday. Mum was getting paid for her first full week of work. Riley was hoping she could give her a little bit of money for Sophie's present.

When Mum picked her up, she was smiling. 'Payday!' she cheered. 'I earned six hundred euros.'

What? Only six hundred euros? The deposit on a crappy apartment was eight hundred euros and you had to pay a month's rent in advance too, so they needed at least sixteen hundred euros to get a place to live, and that was just the awful places.

If her mum was earning six hundred euros a week, it would take three weeks to earn enough money to find a place to live. And that only left two hundred euros for food and petrol. Riley wanted to cry. She thought Mum would be earning more money. Then again, she was washing dishes, so she probably earned the least of all the restaurant staff. But two more weeks in the car? Two whole weeks until they could afford a crappy, smelly flat? Riley felt sick. There was no way she could ask her mum for money for Sophie's present now.

Mum squeezed her arm. 'I'm going to treat you to McDonald's. We can get a cheap meal deal. I'll have to save the rest of my wages, though. We'll have to make the restaurant food that Maja gives us last us for all our meals. We need to be really careful with money. The more we can save, the sooner we'll get our own place.'

Great, leftovers for breakfast, lunch and dinner. Riley knew her mother was trying so hard to be cheerful and she wanted to be happy for her, but she just couldn't get excited. Even when they did have enough money saved, the only apartment they could afford was a disgusting one. Life was just rubbish. Everything was rubbish.

'Hey, cheer up,' said her mum. 'I'll get you a milkshake too if you want?'

Riley shook her head. 'It's OK, Mum, I'm not hungry,' she lied. 'I shared Sophie's lunch and it was huge.'

'Are you sure? I'd like to treat you.'

'Yes, sure.' Riley couldn't eat anything anyway. Her stomach was twisted into tight knots. She felt like vomiting. *How did life get so bad? Will it ever get better?*

'OK, well, we can save that money too, then.' Mum turned the car around and headed back to the restaurant.

While Riley was sitting in the car alone, trying to do her homework, she racked her brains to think of something she could give Sophie. But there was nothing. She cuddled Tiger, then put her head into her hands and sobbed. She hated her life. She hated every single second of her rotten life.

Sophie linked her arm through Riley's at school the next morning. 'Today's the day! Are you excited?'

Riley would normally be upside down with excitement, but today she just felt sick. Sick because she was living in a car, sick because she was starving and sick because she had no present. But she had to fake it.

'OMG, yes, super-excited. I barely slept last night!' That part at least was true. She *had* barely slept. Her mum had a cold and snored all night long. Riley kept waking up to her loud snores. Every time she woke up, she'd start panicking about her life and it would take ages to get back to sleep again. At five o'clock, she'd given up and read her book.

Vanessa came bounding over. 'Hiiiiiii! Today's the big day, then! I cannot *wait* for you to see my present.'

'Me too!' Sophie clapped her hands.

'Mum is going to drop mine over later – it's way too big to bring into school. Did you bring yours in, Riley?'

'No.' Riley had decided, at three in the morning, that she would have to lie. 'I ordered it online but it hasn't arrived on time – it got stuck or something.'

'Where did you order it from?' Vanessa asked.

'America,' Riley lied.

'What is it? Clothes?'

'I can't say. It's a surprise.'

Vanessa looked annoyed. 'Whatever. We'll see it when it arrives – if it ever does.'

'Don't worry, Riley, it'll be nice to get something later on when all the fuss is over,' Sophie said.

Riley smiled at her friend. Oleg passed them in the hall. He glanced sideways at Riley but said nothing.

That afternoon was so boring: maths, science and history. Riley tried not to fall asleep, but her eyes kept drooping. She had to be upbeat for Sophie's party. She couldn't let her friend down by being tired and grumpy.

'Only half an hour to go,' Sophie whispered as the clock on the wall said half-past two.

Riley smiled at her. 'Can't come soon enough!'

'I had to bring Dad shopping for all the treats,' Sophie whispered. 'Mum's been driving me mad. She keeps saying I'm secretly eating full packets of chocolate fingers and tubes of Pringles from the cupboard and that I'm going to have spots and rotten teeth if I don't stop. But it wasn't me who ate them, it's obviously the boys, though they swore it wasn't them. It's *so* annoying.'

Riley looked down at her book and let her hair cover her face like a curtain. She could feel her cheeks burning in shame. She had got her best friend into trouble by stealing from her.

Thankfully Sophie didn't notice Riley's guilty face.

'Anyway, I took Dad shopping and we got tons of stuff. I even made sure to get loads of peanut M&M's because I know they're your favourite.'

Riley squeezed her friend's hand. 'Thanks, Sophie, you're the best.' She tried to concentrate on what Miss Caroline was saying about the Vikings, but all she could think about was Trisha blaming Sophie for eating all those treats when it was Riley who had stolen them. She was a terrible friend. She'd make it up to Sophie by being super fun tonight.

Chapter 10

Sophie and Riley sat at the kitchen counter, cutting strawberries for the chocolate fountain. Trisha stood opposite them, piling cupcakes onto a beautiful cake stand. The cupcakes were covered in baby-pink, lilac and cream butter icing. The icing was sprinkled with tiny chocolate kisses.

Riley's mouth watered. They looked so delicious. All she had eaten today was a few dry crackers for breakfast. She'd stayed in the classroom at lunch time, pretending she had to do her geography homework. Her stomach was rumbling. When Trisha and Sophie weren't looking, she popped a strawberry into her mouth and savoured the sweetness.

'What time are the others arriving?' Trisha asked.

'In an hour,' Sophie said, 'and everything has to be perfect.'

'Don't worry, it will be,' her mother reassured her.

'Where are the boys?' Riley asked, hoping they were away for the night, for Sophie's sake.

'Sophie's dad has taken them to the cinema and then out for pizza, so they won't be back for ages.'

Almost as soon as the words were out of Trisha's mouth, the front door burst open and Brian stormed into the kitchen, his face red with fury. 'They are out of control, Trisha! Something needs to be done.'

'What's happened now?'

'We were asked to leave the cinema.'

'Why?'

'Because,' Brian said, through gritted teeth, 'our genius sons decided that it would be really funny to moon at the row behind us.'

'What's moon? What did they do?' Sophie asked, almost in tears at the thought of her brothers being back home for her party.

'Mooning means they pulled their pants down and flashed their asses at the poor unfortunate people in the row behind us. There was an older lady who actually screamed with the fright of it,' Brian explained.

Riley felt a giggle rising up. She coughed to hide it.

'Oh, for goodness' sake! What is this obsession with the boys and their bottoms?' Trisha shook her head.

'Where are they now?' Sophie's lower lip was wobbling.

'I've locked them in the car.'

Trisha's eyes widened. 'It looks like they've escaped ...'

The four boys came tumbling into the kitchen, giving each other dead arms and wrestling.

'STOP IT NOW!' Trisha roared.

They stood still and looked at her.

'I heard you almost gave some poor woman a heart attack in the cinema, showing off your bottoms.'

The boys sniggered.

'This is *not* funny. You embarrassed your father and yourselves. From now on you are to keep your pants on and I want no more flashing or Supergluing. If I see a bare bum, I will whack it with this spoon here.' Trisha waved a wooden spoon at them.

'That's child abuse,' Tim said.

'No it isn't, Tim, it's called the last resort.'

While she was talking, Ted stuck out his hand and grabbed a cupcake, which he promptly shoved into his mouth. It was too big, so some of it was still sticking out as he chewed. He had lilac icing all over his chin.

'Muuuuuuum!' Sophie pointed at him.

Ted coughed and spluttered as he tried to chew and swallow the bun at the same time. Trisha went over to thump him on the back, afraid he'd choke. While she was focused on Ted, the other three grabbed a cupcake each, and Fred and Tim sprinted out of the room. But then Tom saw the chocolate fountain in the corner of the kitchen and stuck his head under it. The chocolate went everywhere – down his front, up his nose and all over the floor.

Brian went over and yanked Tom up, and ended up covered in chocolate sauce too. 'Will you behave for once in your lives?!' he shouted.

Sophie stood up and screamed, 'I hate you! I hate you all. You're ruining my party. I wish I was an only child. I wish I was Riley.'

No you don't, Riley thought. *I'd take this mayhem any day of the week. It's a bit nuts, but it's fun too.*

'Calm down, pet,' Trisha said. 'The boys will go into the TV room now and behave.'

'They never behave,' Sophie sobbed.

'They will. Your dad will sort it out.' Trisha glared at Brian.

'Me?' Brian was wiping chocolate sauce off his shirt with a tea towel.

'Yes, Brian, you.'

'How?'

Trisha went over to him and whispered. Riley could just hear her. 'Bribe them if you have to – money, a new video game, whatever it takes, just sort it out before Sophie has a nervous breakdown here.'

Brian went off to try and control his sons while Trisha and Riley cleaned up the chocolate mess. Sophie sat on a stool at the counter, crying.

'Thanks, Riley, you're a star for helping. I bet your mum is glad she only has one child. I envy her. I love my boys, but sometimes …' Trisha sighed.

What was it about this family envying Riley? If only they knew how unbelievably rubbish her life was. This family had no idea of the awful situation

Riley and her mum were in – and Riley intended to keep it that way.

They used up a whole kitchen roll to scoop up all the spilt chocolate, then Trisha got out the mop. 'OK, come on now, Sophie, enough crying. It's all cleaned up and sorted now, thanks to Riley's help. Go upstairs and get ready, girls. The spa people will be here in a few minutes and they need to set up.'

Riley took Sophie's arm and they went upstairs to get ready. Riley wet two cotton pads with cold water and placed them on Sophie's swollen, red eyes. 'Lie down for a minute and let them de-puff your eyes,' she said to Sophie.

Riley lay down beside Sophie on her big soft bed. She didn't allow herself to close her eyes. She knew if she did that she would drift off into the deepest sleep. Although Riley wanted to sleep more than anything, she had to stay awake for her friend.

Sophie sat up after a few minutes. 'Thanks, Riley, I feel better now. Thanks for helping to clean up, too. I know I was a bit of a drama queen, but my brothers wreck everything and I want tonight to be perfect. It's my birthday and birthdays should be special.'

Riley didn't even want to think what her birthday would be like next year. Would she still be living in a car? A mouldy apartment? On a restaurant floor? In a car park? Where would she be? Would she even have money for a birthday treat? She pushed the thoughts from her mind.

'Will you help me with my make-up?' Sophie asked. 'I know we're getting it done professionally, but I want to look good when everyone arrives.'

Riley helped Sophie make up her face and was very pleased with the results. You couldn't tell that Sophie had been bawling her eyes out; she looked all sparkly and fresh.

'You look fab, Sophie. It's going to be an amazing party. Everyone is so excited. Let's have the best night ever.'

'I was so looking forward to it, but the boys have ruined it. Now my face is all blotchy.'

'No it isn't, look, the make-up hides all that. You look gorgeous.'

Sophie leant in to the mirror to get a closer look at herself. 'You did a good job. I do look better,' she sighed, 'I just feel flat now – I'm not excited anymore.'

'Come on, we're going to have a great time.' Riley put on some music and began to dance around. She was so tired she wanted to lie down on Sophie's beautiful soft bed and sleep, but she had to be upbeat for her friend.

It's kind of ironic, she thought. *Here am I cheering Sophie up, when the only 'worry' she has is that her brothers are annoying!* Riley blocked out those thoughts, plastered a big smile on her face and got her friend up to dance.

Soon, Sophie was smiling and jumping around. The doorbell rang.

'Oh no. We haven't done your make-up yet,' Sophie said, 'and the others are here now.'

Riley shrugged. 'It's fine, don't worry.' Riley really didn't care about putting on make-up. Two weeks ago she would have been really into it, but there were more important things than make-up when you were homeless.

As Sophie was about to run downstairs, she turned to hug Riley. 'Thanks for making me feel better. You really are the best friend ever.'

Vanessa, Grace and Zoe trooped in through the front door. They were all dressed up and holding beautifully wrapped gifts. Riley's heart sank. How was she going to sort out a gift for Sophie with no money? She'd have to figure something out.

Grace's and Zoe's gifts were a mixture of lip glosses, fluffy socks, body moisturisers, face masks and sweets. Sophie thanked and hugged them both warmly. Vanessa's gift was in a huge Juicy Couture box with a big bow on it. Inside was a gorgeous baby-blue tracksuit and three different T-shirts to wear with it – white, pink and lilac.

Sophie squealed and threw her arms around her cousin. 'I love it,' she said pulling on the soft hoodie.

'I knew you would.' Vanessa smirked.

Riley kind of wished the floor would open up and swallow her. But Sophie turned and hugged her too. 'You being here to help set things up and calm me down was the best.'

They all went into the kitchen. While they had been upstairs, Trisha had hung up a huge glittery *Happy Birthday* banner, and big bunches of helium balloons were floating all over the kitchen. The lights were turned down low and there were five big, comfy chairs lined up against the wall with foot spas and towels beside each one. Scented candles were flickering on the kitchen counter and the smell was amazing.

Five beauticians in pink tunics welcomed them and asked them all to take off their shoes and socks and sit back and relax.

The girls sat side by side giggling while they had their feet and hands soaked, massaged and painted. Riley felt uncomfortable. The beauticians were of mixed ages. Two were probably her mum's age and the other three were a bit younger, but they were still grown-ups. It felt weird having older women massaging her feet and painting her toes. Riley felt spoiled and a bit embarrassed.

'I want purple nail varnish, and also silver stars on each of my toes,' Vanessa said, without a please or a thank you.

Riley went for turquoise with gold sparkles, while Sophie went for baby pink with silver half-moons.

'Excuse me, but the stars aren't all in the exact centre of my toenail,' Vanessa's shrill voice said. 'The one on my second toe is lower than the one on my third toe. I asked you to put them all in the centre.'

Riley looked over at the woman doing Vanessa's toes. She was about the same age as Riley's mum. Riley thought of her mum washing dishes in a restaurant and how disgusted she would be if anyone spoke to her like that. How dare Vanessa be so rude? Everyone deserved respect, no matter what job they did.

There was silence in the room and then Riley heard words coming out of her mouth: 'Don't be so rude, Vanessa. We are so lucky to be here having this amazing experience – stop complaining about everything.'

Vanessa glared at her. 'Shut up, Saint Riley. I wasn't being rude. If you ask for something and it's done wrong, you're allowed to complain. We're the customers here.'

'No, Vanessa, we're the guests,' Riley reminded her.

'Well, I love mine,' Zoe said. 'Look, guys, I went for unicorn blue with tiny little silver unicorns.' Zoe wiggled her toes and everyone laughed. The mood in the room lifted.

'I love mine too,' Riley said. 'Thank you so much,' she said to the lady, who winked at her.

'Me too.' Sophie wiggled her toes as well.

'Forget about it,' Vanessa snapped at the lady doing

her toes. 'I'll just go to a proper salon tomorrow and have mine redone.'

Riley gripped the arms of her chair. She felt a hand on her leg. She looked down. The lady doing her nails whispered, 'Ignore her. She's an idiot.'

After the nails, they each had their hair curled and their make-up done. Vanessa complained about everything. Her hair was too curly, then it was too flat. Her make-up was awful; she could do a better job herself.

Eventually Sophie snapped, 'Fine then, if everything is so awful, maybe you should just call your mum and go home.'

Riley grinned. She knew Vanessa wouldn't want to go home and that Sophie snapping at her would actually bother her.

'Jeez, Sophie, I'm just saying that the quality of the make-up they're using is bad. It's fine, I just think they could use better brands. It's not your fault.'

'Let's all have a great night,' Riley said, changing the subject. 'This is the best party I've ever been to – thanks, Sophie.'

Grace and Zoe whooped in agreement. 'Me too!' they said in unison.

Sophie smiled and Vanessa gave a half-hearted, 'Yeah.'

Trisha came in and told them the disco party bus had arrived. Riley was feeling dizzy with tiredness, but hoped the disco bus would give her another bolt of energy.

The minibus was parked in the driveway. The door was pulled right back and they could see flashing lights and hear blaring music.

The four boys were dancing about in front of the minibus shouting, 'I'm Sophie and this is my, like, OMG, fab, amazeballs party and these are my, like, OMG, best friends foreeeeeeever!' Brian was trying to pull them back into the house.

'Just ignore them,' Riley whispered to Sophie.

'OK, girls, run,' Trisha shouted. The girls ran to the bus and the driver slammed the door shut. Tom tried to jump in but Brian tackled him to the ground. The driver took off at speed, leaving tyre marks on the drive behind him.

'Oh my God, I'm so sorry. I'm so embarrassed about my brothers,' Sophie said, cringing.

'Why?' asked Grace. 'Mine is way worse. He farted on my pillow last night just before I went to bed and thought it was hilarious. Teenage boys are so gross.' She sighed.

'Sisters are a pain, too. Mine never lets me borrow any of her clothes and she tells me that my clothes are lame and dorky,' Zoe joined in.

'Urgh, I'm so glad I'm an only child,' Vanessa said. 'No one touches my stuff or farts on my pillow. That is actually so disgusting, Grace. I am never coming to a sleepover at your house.'

'Yeah, you and Riley are so lucky,' Sophie said.

You are the lucky ones, Riley wanted to scream. *Stop complaining about your 'annoying' siblings. You all have dads and homes and food and heating and showers and toilets and washing machines and cookers and kettles and toasters and beds and couches and chairs and tables …*

The driver cranked up the music and slowed down so they could all dance. Sophie pulled Riley up. 'Let's dance!'

Riley didn't really feel like it, but she jumped up, whooped and joined in, using up every last scrap of energy she had.

CHAPTER 11

Later that evening, back at Sophie's house, Riley sat at the kitchen table and ate and ate and ate.

'Wow, Riley, that's a lot of sugar,' Zoe said. 'Where do you put it all? You're so skinny!'

'Riley's on some crazy diet where she doesn't eat during the day any more,' Vanessa said. 'She keeps saying she's had a big breakfast but I hear her stomach grumbling, so she obviously eats nothing all day.'

Riley wanted to punch Vanessa. She put down the cupcake she had been about to eat.

Zoe's eyes widened. 'For real? Riley that's really dangerous. Your body needs food.'

'I do eat during the day,' Riley said, trying not to blush.

'Not lately, you don't,' Vanessa said. 'You haven't eaten lunch in over a week.'

'I just don't like the sandwiches my mum makes me, but I *do* eat breakfast, a big one.'

'So why does your stomach grumble in the morning, then?' Vanessa kept digging.

Riley really hated her right now.

'I guess I have a grumbly stomach. What's the big deal?'

'You do look very skinny, Riley,' Zoe said. 'My mum says it's bad to be too skinny.'

'Yeah, well, you don't have to worry about that,' Vanessa said nastily. Zoe had developed breasts earlier than the others and looked more curvy as a result.

Zoe crossed her arms to cover her chest.

'I think you're gorgeous, Zoe, and I agree with your mum. I wish I wasn't so skinny,' Riley said.

Zoe smiled gratefully at her.

'Me too,' Sophie said. 'I can't wait to be able to wear a bra and look older.'

'I'm bored,' Vanessa said, wanting to get the attention back. 'Let's watch a horror movie.'

'I'm not sure ...' Zoe said.

'OK, but if it gets really scary, I'm out,' Grace said.

'I hate scary movies,' Sophie said.

'Come on, Sophie,' Vanessa urged. 'Don't be such a baby! It'll be fun. We're all together, so it won't be so frightening. I downloaded one on my iPad. Let's go upstairs – I'm full and too much sugar is bad for you, anyway.'

As they left the kitchen, Riley grabbed a handful of Percy Pigs to hide in her backpack. She didn't feel guilty because it wasn't stealing this time: the sweets were there for all the guests.

The girls trooped upstairs and changed into their gorgeous silk pyjamas. Vanessa pulled out her iPad and pressed play. The girls gathered around, but Riley was beyond exhausted, and besides, she was living in a horror movie, so she didn't need to watch one. She lay down on the blow-up mattress.

'Riley?' Vanessa snapped. 'What are you doing? We're watching a movie. You can't go to sleep. You're such a party pooper.'

Riley decided she had a choice – to blow up at Vanessa or to completely ignore her. She decided to bite her tongue and ignore her. She snuggled up in the bed on the floor. Riley wished she had Tiger to cuddle up to, but she could never let Vanessa see that she still slept with a cuddly toy. She'd definitely make fun of her for that. Riley closed her eyes and fell into a deep sleep.

Ping. Eyes open. Riley woke up from another nightmare, her heart pounding. Where was she? She looked around and saw the sleeping bodies of her friends. Phew, she was safe. She was in Sophie's house.

She lay back down and stared at the ceiling. *Please God, please may Mum earn enough money soon to get us an apartment and please may it not be in a basement and cold and damp and full of mould on the walls.*

Riley tried to get back to sleep but she couldn't. Her mind was whizzing. She hoped her mum was OK in the car alone. She was worried about her; she looked so tired all the time and her hands were red and raw from washing dishes. Riley decided she'd ask Maja if she could help her mum out on the weekends.

Riley was also worried about her schoolwork. She was getting her homework done in the library after school, but her concentration was so bad that she couldn't remember anything. She had done terribly in the Friday test yesterday. Whenever she tried to remember what she had learned, her mind went completely blank.

Riley closed her eyes and tried to bring up her dad's face. She was beginning to forget what he looked like. She took out her phone and flipped through photos of happier times. Her dad had been at work most of the time. He was always gone early and home late, but when he was there, he was great. He always told Riley she was the most important person in his life. And he told her that she could be anything, achieve anything and be successful if she worked hard, was smart and took risks.

But Dad had worked hard and he'd lost everything. 'Reckless' was what Riley had heard the accountant say to Mum. She'd looked up the word; it meant doing something dangerous and not worrying or caring about the results.

Why, Dad? Why *were you reckless?* Why *did you lose all our money?* Why *did you leave us and make us homeless?* Riley missed her dad but she was also angry with him. It was his fault Mum was scrubbing pots and pans and his fault they were living in their stupid car and his fault that her life was now so awful.

Riley turned her head into her pillow and cried silently. Was it wrong to love and hate someone at the same time? She loved her dad but she hated him too. And right now, she hated him more than she loved him.

The other girls woke up at nine and chatted sleepily in their silk pyjamas. Riley didn't want to leave. She wanted to move in with Sophie forever. She wanted her old life back, her old bedroom and house and all the things she had taken for granted.

Riley was first to have a shower. She had a long, hot one. She washed her hair with Sophie's posh shampoo and conditioner and lathered her lemongrass-and-cedarwood shower gel all over her body. It smelled so delicious.

Eventually Grace started banging on the door for her to hurry up. 'Riley! You've been in there for ages.'

Riley reluctantly stepped out and dried herself with a warm, fluffy towel from the heated towel rail. She had never truly appreciated how amazing a hot shower was. She wouldn't take it for granted again.

They all got dressed, packed up and went down to have breakfast and head home. Riley would have to take two buses to get to the restaurant. Mum couldn't collect her because she had to work all day Saturday. She was dreading spending the day in the car on her own.

Sophie went to get the party bags for everyone but couldn't find them. 'Mum, where are the party bags?'

Trisha looked confused. 'I left them in the laundry room.'

'They're not there,' Sophie said.

They heard roaring from the TV room.

'You got the cream in my eye, you fool!' Tim shouted.

Sophie looked at her mother. 'Oh no … Mum, please no.'

They all followed Sophie as she ran to the TV room and threw open the door.

Tim, Tom, Fred and Ted were lying on the couch. They each had a green face mask on and an eye mask over their eyes. Their feet were covered in foot cream, and they had lit the five different scented candles.

'Boys!' Trisha roared.

'Shhhh, Mum, we're relaxing here,' Tim said.

Ted peeped from under his eye mask. 'This stuff smells really good.'

'My feet feel all tingly.' Fred wiggled his toes.

'The candles stink a bit,' Tom complained.

'That's it, I'm moving in with Riley. I am not staying here another minute. I hate you all.' Sophie stormed out of the room and ran upstairs to pack.

Riley froze.

Trisha ushered them all out of the room. 'I'm so sorry, girls. I'll make up new bags for you, and Sophie can bring them into school on Monday.' Turning to Riley she said, 'Riley, do you think your mum would mind if Sophie stayed the night at yours tonight? I think she needs a break from her brothers.'

Riley's mind raced. 'Uhm, well, the thing is, Mum's working today and I, uhm … well I'm staying with … with my uncle tonight because she has to work late.'

'Working late on a Saturday – those employers must be tough,' Trisha said.

'What does she do, exactly?' Vanessa asked.

'She's, like, a customer-service person and stuff,' Riley tripped over her words. Vanessa was watching her closely.

'My mum works most Saturdays too,' Zoe said.

'Seems odd that your mum has to work so late,' Vanessa said, staring at Riley. 'Anyway, Sophie can stay with me, Trisha. I'd love to have her over and my mum will be there all day and night.'

'I'm really sorry I can't help, Trisha.' Riley was almost in tears.

Trisha hugged her. 'Don't you worry a bit, pet. Isn't your mum great to be out working?'

Sophie came back downstairs with a small suitcase. 'OK, Riley, let's go.'

Before Riley could explain, Vanessa stepped forward. 'Riley said no, something about her mum working late. So you're coming to mine, it'll be fab. A private cousin-only sleepover.'

Sophie's face dropped. 'Really? Can I not come to yours, Riley?'

Riley looked down at the ground.

'No, you can't. Alison is out working, fair play to her, so you'll have to go home with Vanessa and stay there. Tanya can tell you all about the new Italian marble tiles she's getting put down in her kitchen,' Trisha said, and then turned her head and rolled her eyes so only Sophie and Riley could see her. Riley suppressed a smile.

Sophie had told Riley that Trisha didn't really like Vanessa's mum, Tanya. She thought she was a terrible snob and Trisha was sorry that her brother had married someone so annoying.

'Sorry, Sophie,' Riley said quietly.

'Whatever, it's fine.' Sophie looked fed up with everything.

Grace's mum arrived and all of the girls, except Riley, got into her car.

'I can drop you home too, Riley?' Grace's mum said.

'Oh no, it's fine, thank you. I'm going to my uncle's house and it's ages away. He's picking me up now from the garage at the end of the road. He just texted me that he had to pop in to get petrol.'

'Are you sure?'

'Yes, thanks.'

As they drove off and Riley picked up her backpack, Trisha gave her another hug. 'I know these past few months have been really tough on you, pet. I lost my dad when I was your age and it's heartbreaking. You are welcome here any time, and if you ever want to talk, I'm here for you. You're a great girl, Riley.'

Riley nodded and turned before Trisha saw the tears in her eyes.

She walked off slowly down the street. Back to the boot of the car.

CHAPTER 12

Maja shook her head. 'Children are not allowed to work until they are sixteen.'

'Oh …'

'I am sorry, Riley. I want to help you. But best way you can help Mummy is to work hard in school. You must be top of class.'

Riley gulped. She had gone from one of the top students in her class to one of the bottom this week. 'I'll try, Maja.'

'You are good kid, Riley. Living in car is not so easy but this will make you strong, like me. Life knocked me back when I was a kid, but it also made me badass.'

Riley smiled. Maja was not someone you would want to mess with. She was small but muscular, with dyed red hair cut into a short bob – she looked like a fighter. She had tattoos all down her arms of angel wings and lots of sayings written in Polish – and one big one down the inside of her left arm in English that read, 'For every dark night there is a brighter day.'

'What happened to you when you were a kid?' Riley asked. She was curious about Maja's past.

Maja sucked her cheeks in. 'Bad things, but I forget about them now. You have to look only to the future, Riley. Looking back is bad. Past is past, future is future. Past we cannot change, future we can. I am happy now. You will be happy too.'

She's right, Riley thought, *you can't change the past but you can change the future. Though I'm only twelve. What can I do to change my future? Only Mum can earn money to pay rent. Only Mum can find us a home.*

Riley felt bad. She was failing at the one thing Maja said she needed to do – being good in school.

'No sad face, come on, the world is not so bad. I will give you special cake that Aleksy made.'

Riley did not want any more cake. She wanted her mum's chocolate cake or her flapjacks, not one of Aleksy's rich cakes. Besides, she was still full from Sophie's party and she had six Percy Pigs in her backpack.

'Thanks so much, Maja, but I'm actually not hungry right now, though thanks for the offer.'

'OK, one more thing,' Maja said. 'When you are older, don't wait for man to look after you. You get big job and buy your own house. No waiting for man.' She wagged her finger. 'You do it for you.'

Riley nodded. Maja was right. Mum had given up everything for Dad and he had let her down. Riley would never rely on a man for anything. She was going to be totally independent like Maja.

'Do not spend money on fancy clothes, fancy cars. Spend on your education, on your house, on your business.'

'Yes.'

'I am in charge of my life and my money. This is important. This is life lesson from me to you.'

'Thank you, Maja.'

Maja reached over and ran her thumb gently in the space between Riley's eyebrows. 'You are getting big line here, Riley. You must not worry so much. Life will get better. Now I'm going to work – customers are coming.'

The restaurant was beginning to fill up, so Riley headed back to the car. She'd try and study using the torch Mum had given her. Riley appreciated Maja's words, but when *would* life get better? In a week? Two? Three? When?

Not knowing what was going to happen was making Riley really anxious. She felt a wave of panic rising up inside her chest so she tried to control her breathing. Riley breathed in for a count of ten and then out again for a count of ten until she felt calmer.

On Monday morning, Riley had a difficult time waking her mum up. She had to shake her really hard and shout at her.

'Mum, I have to be in school by half seven! Wake up!'

Alison tried to open her eyes but then closed them again, like it was too much effort. Riley pulled up her mum's left eyelid. 'I'm sorry, Mum, but you *have* to get up! I need to go to the toilet badly.'

Riley unlocked the gate of the small restaurant car park while her mum dragged herself round to the front of the car and climbed into the driving seat. She slumped against the steering wheel and started the engine.

Mum drove very badly. She swerved a few times and hit the kerb twice. Riley held her breath for most of the journey to school, but thankfully Mum didn't crash the car and Riley got to school just in time to sprint through the door, past Oleg and into the bathroom.

As she was in the cubicle, she heard footsteps outside. Damn, she'd left her wash bag and towel beside one of the sinks. *Please God, don't be a teacher or student.* How could she explain why she had a towel, toothbrush, toothpaste, deodorant and soap in school?

Riley waited for the footsteps to go, then peered out from behind the cubicle door. There on the counter was a carrier bag. Riley looked inside. It contained a box of Weetabix, a carton of milk, a bowl and a spoon. There was a note beside it:

Bring back to Oleg when you're finished.

He knew. Oleg knew that she didn't have any breakfast. Riley was embarrassed. She didn't want Oleg telling the teachers or, worse, the headmistress.

She washed her face, put on some deodorant, brushed her teeth and went to find him.

He was in the big school storage cupboard.

Riley knocked on the half-open door.

Oleg looked up. 'Come in,' he said, smiling at her.

The cupboard was actually very big. It was full of cleaning products, broken desks, old sports equipment, tools for fixing things, drills, brushes … There was a space towards the back that was big enough for Oleg to have a little table and stool in the corner. He had a kettle, a little fridge and a microwave in there too.

'Sorry to disturb you. I think you left this for me, but I don't need it, thank you. I had breakfast already. I have it early, so I'm fine, really. And if you're wondering about the whole towel and toothbrush thing, that's just because … because …' Riley tripped over her words. 'Well, you see, our shower is broken, so I have to do all that here, but it'll be fixed really soon. We're getting a whole new bathroom installed and it's going to be lovely. So … there's no need to say anything to anyone. I won't be coming in early again – it's all fine.' She began to back out of the room.

Oleg called her back. 'Please. Don't be embarrassed. I know you are hungry. I can see it in your eyes. Sit down, eat. You're safe here. I won't tell anyone.' He pulled out a small stepladder and indicated for Riley to sit on it.

'I'm not, honestly, you're wrong. I had … I had

bacon, and toast, and … and scrambled eggs. Yum.'

Oleg shook his head. 'You don't need to pretend with me.'

'I'm not pretending.'

He looked directly at her and raised his eyebrows.

Riley felt the fight drain from her body. She'd had another awful night's sleep and she really was hungry.

'OK,' she said quietly. 'Thank you, Oleg.'

She poured herself a bowl of milk and added one Weetabix. Oleg took two more out and plonked them into her bowl. 'You need to fill up for the day.'

Riley ate hungrily. 'Where does the name Oleg come from?' she asked.

Oleg smiled. 'I'm from Moldova, if that's what you're asking. I came here when the school I was working in was shut down and I couldn't find another job.'

Riley nodded. 'Were you a caretaker in a school there?'

'No, I was an English teacher.'

Riley's mouth dropped. 'What? But how …? I mean, why …?'

'Why am I working as a caretaker?'

Riley reddened.

'I came to Ireland because things were very bad in Moldova, and because my cousin was here and he said it was a nice place to come and that there were jobs and they paid well. I earn more as a caretaker here than I did as a teacher there.'

'Wow, that's crazy. Where exactly *is* Moldova?' Riley had no clue where it was. She'd never even heard of it.

'Moldova is a small country squashed between Romania and Ukraine. It's a beautiful place, but it's hard to make a living there.'

'I'm sorry you had to leave your country.'

He smiled sadly. 'Me too. I miss my family. But I send home money so my kids can go to a good school and my wife can pay for the house. Hopefully, I will go home and be with them again before too long.'

Oh my God, Riley thought, *his wife and kids are over there. Poor Oleg.* 'What age are your kids?'

'My son is eight and my daughter is about your age, eleven.'

'I'm just twelve. Gosh, you must miss them.'

'Every day.' He smiled sadly again.

'How long have you been in Ireland?' Riley asked.

'Three years.'

'Without going back to visit? Wow, Oleg, that must be so hard.'

'I do visit, but only in the school holidays. It's hard being apart, but I want my family to have a good life, so it's worth it. Besides, the people here in Ireland are, mostly, very nice.'

Oleg was just like Mum, working in a difficult job to pay for a home and a better life for his kids.

Oleg sat back and crossed his arms. 'Now, tell me about you. What's really going on?'

Riley rubbed her eyes. She was sick of lying and pretending. Oleg had been honest with her, so she was going to be honest with him.

She told him the whole story. She didn't leave anything out. Her dad, the business, the house, the empty bank accounts … she even told him about how her mum hadn't spoken to her own parents since they'd refused to come to her wedding. Riley had never even met them. She told him how her mum never, ever talked about them and that the only uncle she had was in rehab.

It felt so good to say the words out loud and not pretend things were fine. It was freeing, to be honest. Riley felt lighter by the time she finished talking.

'That is very hard for you, Riley, I'm sorry. Your mother sounds like a very special person.'

Riley nodded. 'She is, but I'm worried about her. She's working so much and she's not used to it. She's tired all the time.'

'We adults are stronger than we look. When it comes to protecting our children, we can do almost anything.'

'But …' Riley was afraid to say what she was thinking. It was her biggest fear. 'What if she gets sick and dies too?'

'Hey, I've seen your mum – she's a strong woman. Don't worry about that. You are going through a difficult time, but it will get better. Your mum will have enough money soon for an apartment. In the meantime, why don't we do this: you come in at seven-thirty, do your bathroom stuff and then come in to me here and have breakfast. What's your favourite cereal?'

'Oh gosh, Weetabix is fine.'

'Riley, answer the question.' He smiled warmly at her.

'Crunchy Nut cornflakes.'

Oleg laughed. 'Well, Miss Riley, tomorrow that is what you shall have for your breakfast.'

They both jumped as they heard footsteps.

Oleg told Riley to wait, then opened the door and peered out. 'It's OK. Whoever it was has gone. You can go now – the corridor is clear.'

Riley shook his hand. 'Thank you, really, from the bottom of my heart, thank you.'

She snuck out the door and skipped off to class, feeling happier than she had in ages. She couldn't wait to tell Mum how kind Oleg was and how he was just like her, working hard to look after his kids. She would be relieved Riley was getting breakfast in school too. Mum had been right that night in Starbucks when she'd said that the kindness of strangers could be very powerful. Riley had seen Oleg around the school for years, but she'd never wondered about his life. She felt bad about that now.

Oleg was beginning to feel like a friend, a lovely, kind friend who understood what Riley and Mum were going through.

CHAPTER 13

Miss Caroline was talking about the class trip to the adventure centre in the west of Ireland that coming Thursday and Friday. She said this was the final reminder to bring in one hundred euros tomorrow for payment. 'Now, make sure you write a reminder in your homework journals. If it hasn't been collected tomorrow, I'm afraid you won't be able to go.'

Zoe gasped. 'Oh no, I forgot the envelope again. I'll definitely bring it in tomorrow, Miss Caroline. I'm going to write it on my hand now.'

'I can't wait,' Sophie said. 'It's going to be so much fun. I hope we get put in the same bedroom,' she said to Riley.

Riley tried to push the lump in her throat down by coughing. 'Mmmmm, yeah, me too.' There was no way Riley could ask her mother for a hundred euros for a school trip. She'd have to lie and make something up. But then if Mum saw she wasn't going to school, she'd ask why, and then she'd get upset that Riley hadn't been able to go on the trip and ... well, Riley really didn't want to upset her.

What was she going to do while her class was off on the trip? She'd have to put her uniform on and pretend to go to school and wander around. Maybe she could find a library near the restaurant and hide out there. But it would be from half-past seven in the morning until six at night, and Mum would be dropping her to and from school. What if one of the teachers spotted Riley and asked her what she was doing, why she wasn't on the school trip? Riley's head throbbed with all the complications of the next few days.

At break-time the girls went to sit under the oak tree.

'Let's co-ordinate our treats so we don't all bring the same stuff,' Sophie said. 'I'll bring jellies, Riley, you bring chocolate and, Vanessa, you bring crisps, OK?'

'I'm dreading it,' Vanessa moaned.

'Why? It's going to be super fun,' Sophie said.

'Ugh, doing mud runs and kayaking in a freezing cold lake sounds horrendous. I'm not wearing the disgusting wetsuits from the adventure centre. Mum bought me my own one at the weekend. It's the best you can get, so hopefully I won't die of cold.'

'I can't wait to go,' Sophie said. 'Can you, Riley?'

'Can't wait.' Riley tried to sound enthusiastic.

'You don't look like you're keen at all,' Vanessa said. 'You look wrecked, Riley. Are you staying up late?'

'Yeah, I was watching Netflix last night for ages,' Riley lied. *I wish,* she thought. *If only you all knew that I was actually stuck in a freezing cold car, crushed up against my mother, waking up every few hours panicking about my future.*

'Go to bed early for the next few nights – we want to be able to stay up late at the adventure camp,' Sophie said.

Riley nodded, avoiding her friend's eyes.

'I'm bringing my own sleeping bag too,' said Vanessa. 'Their duvets will be disgusting. And my own shampoo

113

and conditioner and hairdryer. And food. I'm not eating revolting chicken nuggets or whatever they serve.'

'Why don't you just not go?' Riley was sick of her moaning.

Vanessa stopped applying her lip gloss and stared at Riley. 'Because I don't want to miss out, obviously. Everyone's going to be banging on about it for weeks after, so I *have* to go.'

'Well, then try to enjoy it,' Sophie said. 'I can't wait to get away from my brothers for a night.'

Riley wished she *could* go. She loved the idea of being with her friends doing adventurous stuff. The sixth-class trip to the adventure centre was something they had looked forward to for months. How was she going to hide not going from absolutely everyone, including her mum?

Mum insisted on coming in and talking to Oleg the next morning. She thanked him for his kindness. Oleg said giving Riley breakfast was only a small thing and that he hoped she would find a place to live soon. He said he'd ask around and see if any of his friends knew of a place for rent. Mum was super grateful and told him he was a very good man.

But when Mum left, Riley couldn't eat anything, because she had begun to worry about the class trip and her stomach was in a big knot.

Oleg watched her push her Crunchy Nut cornflakes around the bowl. 'What's wrong?'

Oleg was the one person that Riley could be totally honest with.

'I can't go on the school trip tomorrow because it costs a hundred euros and I can't tell my mum because she'll be upset that we can't afford it. I have to pretend to Sophie that I'm sick and to my mum that I'm going to school as normal.'

Oleg took a sip of his strong black coffee. Riley didn't know how he was able to drink it: it looked like black ink.

'OK, let's break this down. You tell your friends you're not feeling too good today and then tomorrow morning you text Sophie and tell her you can't go because you are sick. You get dressed in your uniform and come to school early and you can spend the day here in the storage room. I know it's cramped and not so comfortable, but I'll find some things for you to sleep on. You need sleep – you are looking very tired. And you can charge your phone

115

here and read and study or watch YouTube or whatever you kids do.'

'Really? Seriously? You'd do that for me?' Riley felt relief flood her body. She wouldn't have to walk the streets hiding from everyone. She could be safe and warm and cosy in here while Oleg was off working.

Oleg smiled at her. 'Of course. People helped me when I came here and I am happy to help you. I hope that if one of my kids was in trouble someone would help them. I believe in karma. If you are kind to others, kindness will come back to you.'

Riley stood up from the stepladder and smiled. 'Thank you so much, Oleg. You are the best.'

Oleg laughed and patted her on the back.

Riley skipped into class feeling so much happier. The only thing she had to do now was tell a white lie to her teacher.

She waited for Miss Caroline at the classroom door. 'Morning, Miss.'

'Good morning, Riley. Did you remember to bring in the money today?'

'The thing is … I can't go. It's my dad's birthday

tomorrow and Mum and I want to celebrate him quietly. If you don't mind, I'm just going to tell my friends that I'm not feeling well. I don't want people asking questions.' Riley felt bad lying about her dad's birthday – it wasn't really until July – but she knew it would stop Miss Caroline asking too many questions.

Her teacher looked concerned. 'I'm so sorry, Riley, that will be a very hard day for you and your mum. I totally understand that you don't want to come on the trip. Don't worry, I'll say nothing. I'm very sorry again. You're a great girl, Riley.'

'Thanks.' Riley smiled inside. Everything was sorted. She'd text Sophie tomorrow saying she had a tummy bug and hide out in Oleg's storeroom instead. Her stomach stopped aching.

At lunch time, Riley unwrapped leftovers from the restaurant.

'Oh my God, that stinks! What is it?' Vanessa wrinkled her nose.

'It's Polish stew – one of the people Mum works with gave it to her. It's delicious.'

'I wouldn't eat that if you paid me. Gross. Why can't your mum give you normal food?'

Riley felt Vanessa's eyes boring into her. 'I like Polish food,' she said.

'My mum says it's good to try new things,' Sophie said.

'*Nice* new things, not revolting things like that!' Vanessa pointed her perfectly painted fingernail at Riley's lunch.

'Some people have nothing to eat, so I'm grateful for what I have.' Riley was sick of Vanessa. It was food, and she was hungry.

'OK, Saint Riley. God, you're turning into such a bore.'

Riley sat on her hands to stop herself from pouring stew all over Vanessa's perfect hair.

'I think we should go back to your house today, Riley. We haven't seen your new place. We can buy the treats for the trip on the way and divide them all up,' Vanessa said.

'I go to after-school study until five,' Riley reminded her.

'Skip it today. We won't have any homework. Call your mum and tell her.'

'She's working. She can't pick me up any earlier.'

'Fine, my mum can bring us, then. Just tell her where you live.'

Riley's heart began to thump in her chest. Why couldn't Vanessa just leave her alone? 'I don't have a key.'

'Yesterday you said you had a key because your mum sometimes worked at the weekends.'

'I left it at home.'

'How come you never invite us to your house?' Vanessa was beginning to sound suspicious. 'We want to see it, don't we, Sophie?'

Sophie shrugged. 'Well, yeah, but only when it suits Riley.'

'But it never suits Riley.'

'Her mum's working really hard, Vanessa. Just drop it,' Sophie said.

'I just think it's weird,' her cousin went on. 'If *I* had a new house, I'd be dying to show it off.'

'Well, I'm not like you,' Riley said, trying hard not to show her anger.

'No one is like me. I'm unique.' Vanessa flicked her hair and smirked.

'That's one word for you!' Sophie rolled her eyes.

Thankfully the bell rang before Riley completely lost her temper and told Vanessa some of the words she could think of to describe her – all of them bad ones.

Chapter 14

Mum was curled in a ball, sleeping so deeply that Riley didn't want to disturb her. She just watched her instead. Mum had shrunk. She'd always been small, but now she looked like a little doll. Her cheeks had hollowed out and her wrists were like a tiny bird's. Her beautiful, thick, bouncy black hair, which she used to get blow-dried at the hairdresser's twice a week, was now greasy and scraggy. Her forehead was covered in a shiny film of sweat. Where had her mum gone?

Mum didn't look like Mum any more. When they'd gone to look at a flat yesterday after she'd picked Riley up, Mum hadn't even tried arguing with the landlord when he'd said the rent had gone up and was no longer the nine hundred euros a month it had said in the ad. Instead it was now eleven hundred euros a month and he had three people after it, so if Mum wanted it she would have to hand over twenty-two hundred euros now to reserve it.

Mum had said nothing, just turned around and climbed back into the car. It was like the light had gone out in her. She had no more fight. Work was sucking her energy dry and there was nothing left to give.

Riley had tried to cheer her up by singing her favourite song, Abba's 'Dancing Queen', on the way home, but instead of cheering her up, it had made Mum cry. She kept saying, 'I'm so sorry, I'm a rubbish mum,' over and over. It made Riley feel really sad. They'd both ended up crying. But then they'd had a big hug and Mum had dried her tears and Riley's and told Riley how much she loved her and how she was going to be a better mum from now on.

Before waking Mum up, Riley sent a text to Sophie: '*Gutted, can't make trip, tummy bug. Puking all night.☹ Enjoy.*'

Sophie replied straight away: '*NOOOOOOO! Please come anyway.*'

'*Can't, too sick.*'

Sophie sent three lines of sad face emojis.

Riley wriggled into her school uniform, giving her mother a few last precious minutes of sleep. But she had to get to school early to hide before any of the teachers saw her. She gently shook her mum's shoulder.

'Mum, sorry, but we have to go.'

Mum didn't move.

Riley shook her a little more. 'Mum, you have to wake up.'

Mum groaned.

'Sorry, Mum, but we have to go.'

Mum peeled her eyes open. 'It's OK, pet, just give me a second.' She struggled to sit up and then began to cough and cough.

At last Mum caught her breath and Riley handed her a cup of water. 'Thanks.' Mum stopped coughing and rubbed her eyes.

She slowly climbed over the back seat and opened the door. They both got out and stretched their tired, aching bodies. Riley unlocked the car park gate. Then Mum got into the front seat and they took off.

'Don't worry, I'll have you there in time for breakfast with Oleg,' Mum said. 'I'm so grateful that he is being so kind to you.'

'Yeah, he's the best.'

'At least I know you get breakfast before school, which makes me feel a tiny bit less like a terrible mother.'

'Mum, you are *not* a terrible mother. Stop saying that. You're working so hard to get us a place. I know we'll get one this weekend – I can feel it in my bones.'

'Aw, Riley, what would I do without you?' Mum pulled up outside the empty school and kissed Riley on the cheek as she got out.

Her mother's cheek felt clammy and hot. 'Try and get some more sleep before work, Mum,' Riley said. 'You need it.'

'Don't worry about me. I'm fine. I've got the best kid in the world.' Mum gave her a weak smile, then waved and drove off.

Riley rushed into the school to use the bathroom and hide. Oleg had made a soft seating area for her in his storeroom. It was just big enough. He'd put a thick gym mat down and found a bean bag. There was a fleecy blanket and a soft pillow too. Everything smelled fresh and clean.

After Riley had eaten a huge bowl of cereal and gone to the bathroom, Oleg told her to rest. 'You are safe here. No one will disturb you. When I come back at lunch time, I'll knock three times so you know it's me before you open the door. OK?'

Riley didn't argue, and, as soon as Oleg had gone off to work, she slumped down on the bean bag, covered herself with the fleecy blanket and fell into a deep sleep.

Oleg came back at lunch time. He knocked three times before coming in.

'I have food for you,' he said, smiling at her. Sitting down opposite her, he said, 'Look, Riley, I am happy to help you out with breakfast, but hiding you in here can only be a one-off, unless you let me talk to the headmistress. If someone found out I was hiding a student in here it could get me into a lot of trouble. I haven't said anything because I know you don't want anyone to know about your situation, and hopefully your mum will find a place soon. But if you are stuck and need to spend the day in school again, we will need to talk to the headmistress, OK?'

Riley nodded. 'I'm so sorry. The last thing I want is for you to get into trouble. I won't have to do this again – once Mum gets us a place to live, I can stay there.'

'Come on, let's eat.' Oleg handed Riley a plate and a knife and fork. 'Today for lunch we are having plăcintă, a traditional Moldovan food. It's like a pancake and I put cheese inside.'

Oleg placed three pancake-type things onto Riley's plate. Riley smiled to herself. She used to be a fussy eater, only liking certain food. Now she was eating Polish and Moldovan food and was grateful for every bite. Even if she didn't like it, she ate it. But these were delicious. They were still warm and the cheese was all melted inside.

In between big bites, Riley thought she should be polite and ask Oleg about his country. Mum always said it was important to show an interest in others. 'Tell me some more about Moldova and your family.'

Oleg's eyes got a bit misty. 'I have a beautiful wife, Galina, who is looking after our kids and working part-time as a nurse. The kids are doing well in school and they seem happy.'

'You must really miss them.'

'I do, very much. We Skype every night but it's not the same. I can't wait to see them and hug them and kiss them.'

'When will you see them next?'

'I'm going home at the end of June for two weeks, when the school closes.'

That was two months away. *Poor Oleg. Imagine not seeing your kids for months and months at a time.* 'Are all Moldovan people as nice as you?' she asked.

He smiled at her. 'We are good people, very hardworking. It's a small country, like Ireland. We have beautiful forests and rivers and long, warm summers, not like here.'

'Lucky you,' Riley said.

'Not so lucky, really. We are one of the poorest countries in Europe.'

'Do you speak Moldovan?'

'Yes, it's very similar to Romanian, and a lot of Moldovans can also speak Russian.'

'And you speak English too. You must be very clever. I'm rubbish at languages. I find French hard. But I googled a Moldovan word.' Riley smiled. '*Multimesec.*'

Oleg clapped his hands and roared laughing. 'Well done.'

Riley grinned. 'I looked it up last night, but I think I said it wrong.'

'Only a little. You pronounce the word for "thank you" as "*Mulţumesc*", so "*Moolt-soo-mesk*".'

Riley repeated it. '*Mooltsoomesk.*'

'Excellent,' Oleg said. 'And you are very welcome.'

He tidied up the food and said he'd check on her later. Riley took out her science book. She should really do some study to catch up. But after eating, she felt tired again, so she took Tiger out of her backpack and snuggled down with him for a little five-minute nap.

Oleg's knocking woke her up three hours later. Riley couldn't believe she had basically slept all day, but she felt so much better. Oleg made her a cup of hot chocolate and Riley sat up on the stool and drank it.

'Have you heard from your friends on the trip?' he asked.

'No, they only get their phones for ten minutes to phone home later.'

'Sophie is your best friend, yes?'

'Yes.'

'Is she a good friend?'

Was Sophie a good friend? Riley used to think so, and most of the time she still did. But Sophie's world was so different to hers now. Sometimes she thought Sophie was a bit blind to the world around her. But then again, had Riley noticed homeless people living in doorways before she became homeless? Did she think about starving kids before she was hungry herself?

'Yes, she is,' she said at last. 'Sophie lives in a bit of a bubble, like I used to. But she's kind and fun. Her cousin Vanessa is a nightmare, though. She joined the school in September and Sophie kind of got stuck with her and so I did too. She's actually a really horrible person.'

It felt good to admit how she really felt about Vanessa, that she kind of hated her. She knew *hate* was a strong word, but there was nothing nice about Vanessa. Not one single thing.

'You need to stay away from horrible people. They are like a poison.'

'I know, but she's Sophie's cousin, so she can't dump her.'

'That's difficult. Maybe try and spend more time with other friends?'

'But then Sophie will feel left out and hurt.'

Oleg rolled his eyes. 'Girls are so complicated. Boys are easy. With boys, you hand them a ball and they all play together.'

Riley laughed. 'You should meet Sophie's four brothers – they're not easy at all, they're out of control!'

Oleg grinned. Riley began to pack up her things and tidy up. She handed the blanket to Oleg. 'I hope you get to go home for good soon. I'd say you're a great dad, and your kids should get to spend more time with you.'

He smiled and she thought she saw a tear in the corner of his eye. 'Thank you, Riley, I hope so too.'

'Family is everything, really, isn't it? At the end of the day, it's all you have.'

Oleg nodded. 'You are a wise girl.'

I didn't used to be, Riley thought. *I used to be worried about what colour to paint my nails, or what top to buy for a birthday party. I've only got wise because my life has been ripped apart. If this is what it takes to be wise, I'd rather be stupid!*

Chapter 15

Riley stood across the road, hidden from sight behind a big tree. Their old house looked exactly the same. Even though it had only been a few weeks since she'd lived there, it felt like a different world. She hadn't realised how big their home was. Five bedrooms for only three people. The new owners had painted the front door red. Riley preferred the old colour – sky blue.

She looked up at what had been her bedroom window. The bedroom she had had sleepovers in. The bedroom Mum had read her stories in. The bedroom Dad had kissed her goodnight in. The bedroom she had played in. The bedroom she had been happy and safe and cosy in. The bedroom she had lived in, not having the faintest idea that there were kids all over the country who were dealing with so much.

Riley thought it was only kids in places like Syria or Ukraine or other countries with wars or famines who were homeless and hungry. She never thought kids in Ireland could be. Riley had googled it, and there were over ten thousand people who were homeless in Ireland. Riley could not believe it. How was the number so high? Ireland was a wealthy country and there was food in all the supermarkets and lots of houses and apartments, so how come so many people were homeless? It didn't make sense.

She'd also looked up 'help for homeless people in Dublin' and lots of websites came up with shelters and hostels to stay in, but Mum said some of them could be a bit dodgy and she thought they were better and safer in the car. Riley wasn't so sure about that. There were also soup kitchens where you could queue up to get food, but Riley would die if anyone saw her there, and besides, they were getting food from the restaurant now.

One of the websites said they were entitled to social welfare payments, but that it was difficult to get the money because you had no address for them to send it to. It was all so complicated it made her head hurt.

The front door of her old house opened and a woman stepped out holding a little girl's hand. They looked so clean and pretty and happy. *Why wouldn't they be happy, they live in a beautiful house*, Riley thought. *My house.* Riley closed her eyes and pictured happier times, sitting in the kitchen on her tenth birthday surrounded by gifts, as Mum brought over a big chocolate cake covered in Smarties and Dad sang 'Happy Birthday' and took photos. Riley could still feel the happiness of that moment.

She opened her eyes and came back to reality. It was not her house anymore and the past was in the past. As Maja said, Riley had to focus on the future now. Riley took one last look, then turned her back on the house and her past and walked away.

Riley kept her head bent low as she passed a big, scary-looking security guard. She was glad she'd worn a baseball cap. She kept her head down and headed to the section where the hoodies were. They were laid out in rows. There were so many different colours. The baby pink one was by far the nicest. Riley knew Sophie would love it. But she had to check first. She went through all the pink ones, but they all had security tags attached to them. She then went through every single other colour until she found one without a tag. It was green, which was not Sophie's favourite colour, but it was still nice. Riley looked around for the dressing rooms. They were in the corner on the left.

Riley grabbed four more random things to try on. The girl in charge of the changing room was distracted, so Riley was able to sneak past her without having to show how many items of clothing she had. Maybe she'd get away with this after all.

She was in the dressing room, sitting down on the little bench, sweating and trying to calm her breathing, when she heard Zoe's voice from the cubicle next door.

'Vanessa thinks something's up with Riley. Like, she was totally fine in school on Wednesday and then she was suddenly too sick to come to the adventure camp.'

'Maybe she's still just really sad about her dad,' Grace said.

'Vanessa said that her mum told her that Riley's dad owed loads of people money and that he never paid any of it back and when he died his business was in big trouble.'

'That's awful. Poor Riley.'

Riley had to use all of her willpower to stop herself from ripping the curtain open and telling Zoe and Grace exactly what she thought of Vanessa. How dare she talk about Dad like that? How dare she be so nasty and spread awful stories?! OK, they were true, but still… … Why did Vanessa have to be such a cow? Riley felt her stomach twist into a knot as she listened.

'I know, and Vanessa thinks that Riley doesn't want us to go back to her house because it's tiny or maybe not even a house at all, maybe just, like, an apartment or something,' Zoe's annoying, squeaky voice continued.

'So what?' Grace said. 'I mean, Vanessa shouldn't be saying those things. She's always been jealous of Riley because she's Sophie's bestie.'

'I don't think she was trying to be mean – she was just asking me if I knew where Riley lived now and if I'd noticed she was being weird,' Zoe said defensively.

How stupid was Zoe? How could she not see Vanessa was being horrible? At least Grace could see through her, thought Riley. At least Grace had defended her.

'Which colour is better? The blue or the red?' Zoe asked, changing the subject.

'They're both fab on you.'

'You know what, I'll get both. Mum just won some, like, really big case in court, so she won't mind.'

Spoiled cow, Riley thought grumpily. *I can't even afford a bar of chocolate.* Riley missed going shopping with Sophie. They used to do it almost every Saturday afternoon after hockey. They'd head to the shopping centre and try on loads of things and take selfies and then buy the outfits they liked best. Riley had never even thought about money then. Her mum had given her a Revolut card and told her to treat herself, within reason. She'd had to give that back as soon as Dad had died.

Riley heard her classmates leaving the changing room. With shaking hands, she pushed the green hoodie into her backpack and waited another few minutes before coming out of her cubicle. She wanted to make sure Grace and Zoe had left the shop.

Her legs trembling, she handed the dressing room attendant four items back and walked out. Riley knew she had to move fast before she lost her nerve. She sped through the shop and out of the front door. The security guard was looking at his phone and paying no attention. Riley held her breath as she walked through the doors, waiting for an alarm to go off, or for someone to grab her. But nothing happened. She kept walking and headed straight for the shopping centre exit.

She gulped in air when she got outside. She had been holding her breath the whole way out. Riley leant against a wall and tried to stop shaking. She had just stolen something from a shop. Now she had stolen from her best friend *and* from her favourite shop. Riley felt sick. What was she turning into? The fact that she had stolen the hoodie as a gift for Sophie didn't make it all right. Riley knew what she had done was wrong and that her mum would be shocked and disgusted with her if she knew.

She began to cry. She just wanted to give her best friend a present. She didn't want to be the only one who hadn't given her anything. Vanessa kept asking when her gift was going to arrive from America. She felt so much pressure. And now she'd done this.

Riley swore she would never, ever steal anything again, no matter what.

CHAPTER 16

Riley stuffed her backpack containing the stolen hoodie under the passenger seat of the car. She didn't want to look at it or think about it. She went into the restaurant via the back door, which brought her straight into the kitchen.

It was four o'clock, the quiet time between shifts. Her mum was the only person in the kitchen. She was leaning against the counter, holding a cloth in one hand and an antibacterial spray in the other. But she wasn't moving. Riley went over to her. Mum's eyes were glazed and her face was red and covered in sweat.

'Mum? Are you OK?' Riley asked.

'Water,' she croaked.

Riley rushed over to the sink and filled a glass with cold water. She handed it to Mum, who raised it to her lips, then suddenly dropped it as she fainted.

'Mum!' Riley screamed.

Maja rushed through the door from her office. 'What's happening?'

She saw Mum on the floor. Riley was cradling her mother's head and crying. Maja crouched down and felt her mum's forehead.

'Is my mum going to die?' Riley cried.

Maja rolled her eyes. 'Nobody is dying, silly girl. Your mummy just has bad temperature. She needs medicine.' She opened a drawer and pulled out a bottle of paracetamol. 'Alison, take these now. Come on, open your mouth.'

Maja pulled Mum up into a sitting position and slapped her gently on the face. Mum opened her eyes. 'Drink and swallow,' Maja ordered.

Alison did as she was told. Riley sat beside her mother, holding her hand and crying.

'No crying. Mummy is OK, she is just needing to rest.'

'I'll go and make up a bed for her in the car,' Riley said.

Maja shook her head. 'No, you are coming to my house tonight. I will make Mummy better.'

Riley was so relieved that Maja was there to help and to give her mum the right medicine. She couldn't believe she was going to let them sleep in her flat. She threw her arms around Maja. 'Thank you.'

'Come on, help me get Mummy up.'

They pulled Mum up and put her in the back of Maja's minivan. Riley went to get her backpack and some clothes and toiletries for her and Mum.

Then Riley sat in the back of the minivan, cuddling her mother. Mum was all she had. If anything happened to her, Riley had no one left. She would be alone in the world. She felt her chest squeeze as she tried to take big breaths.

Mum stroked Riley's cheek. 'I'm sorry, sweetie. Don't worry, I just feel very tired. I'll be fine.'

'Please get better, Mum, please.'

'Of course I will.'

'Don't leave me, Mum,' Riley cried.

'Hey, it's just a little flu, I'll be fine. Oh, Riley, I'm sorry I scared you. I love you, angel.'

Riley buried her head into her mother's neck and cried.

Maja lived ten minutes from the restaurant in a big concrete block of apartments. She was on the ninth floor. There was graffiti all over the walls of the outside. They got the lift up and inside the apartment was lovely.

Maja had painted the walls a sunflower yellow and the old couches were covered in colourful throws. It was small, but everything was neat and tidy. Everything had its own place. There was only one bedroom, so Maja got Riley to help her pull out the sofa bed in the main room, then together they made it up with fresh sheets that smelled of spring.

Mum crawled into the bed and Riley covered her with a duvet. She and Maja watched as she fell into a deep sleep.

'She will be sleeping a lot, but this is good for temperature. In four hours you give her two more tablets. OK?' Maja handed Riley the bottle of tablets. 'Also, you cool her face with this.' She handed Riley a damp, cool facecloth. Riley nodded.

'I have to go now. You find food in kitchen, you eat it. I will call later.'

'Thank you so much, Maja,' Riley said.

'No problem – you are good girl. You look after Mummy.'

Maja left, and Riley lay down beside her mother and watched her sleep. She wondered if this was her punishment for stealing. Was this God's way of showing her what happens when you commit a crime?

Riley's head throbbed. She closed her eyes and fell asleep, snuggled beside her mother – her only family and her world.

The next morning, Mum's temperature was down and she was able to sit up in bed and eat a small bit of toast and drink a cup of tea.

'Thank you, Maja, for letting us stay. That's the best sleep I've had in months,' Mum said, smiling weakly at her employer.

'You are needing rest. You are needing proper apartment.'

'We're due to see five more today,' Mum said.

'You are still sick – you are not going to see apartments. I will go with Riley,' Maja said.

'Oh no, Maja, it's your only day off,' Mum protested.

Maja shrugged. 'You need to get better so you can work. I do not have any plans today, only doing laundry.'

Riley sat beside Maja in the front of the minivan as Maja drove to the first address. Riley clung to the door handle as Maja drove fast through the streets. She drove right up behind whatever car was in front of her, almost touching their boot, honking her horn at cyclists and people crossing the road too slowly.

Riley was glad to get out of the car when they arrived at the first apartment.

The owner of the apartment stood at the door, asking for everyone's names and telephone numbers as they walked in.

'I am not giving my name or number. If I like apartment, *then* I give my name and number. If I don't like, I don't give,' Maja said, attempting to push past the big man.

'The rent has gone up. It's nine hundred and fifty a month now.'

Maja glared at him. 'What do you mean? You said eight hundred fifty in ad.'

'Yeah, well, as you can see, a lot of people have come to see it, so the rent is going up.'

Maja elbowed her way in, Riley following. 'Excuse me,' Maja said loudly to the six other people viewing the apartment. 'This man said rent is eight hundred fifty. Now he says nine hundred fifty. This is not OK. This is cheating. This is not fair. Landlords are bullies. We need to say no. Nobody here say they pay more than eight hundred fifty. Then it will be fair.'

The other people stared at her.

'I agree with you, love,' a woman with a baby in her arms said, 'but I've looked at thirty-six flats in the last three weeks. I have to do whatever it takes to get a place to live. If I have to pay more, then I will. I'll be homeless otherwise.'

'But if we let landlords change prices like this, we let them bully us!' Maja said.

A man beside Riley sighed. 'What can we do? We need a place to live. If we don't pay up, we'll be on the streets.'

'He is a bad man,' Maja spat. 'We must fight back!'

'You're a troublemaker – out you go,' the landlord said, trying to push Maja out the door. But he had no idea who he was dealing with. Maja shoved him back.

'Do not push me! I will call the police if you touch me. You are not bullying *me*, mister. I am not afraid of you.'

'Why don't you piss off back to wherever you came from?' the landlord hissed.

'I live here, I work here, I employ people here – Riley's mummy works for me – I am helping this country. What are you doing, fat man? You are ripping people off. I would not live here for one euro a month.'

'Get out, then!' he shouted.

'I am happy to go.' Maja grabbed Riley's hand and stormed out of the flat, the other viewers watching her go with their mouths open.

Riley thought of her mum and how polite and meek she was. Mum would never have pushed a man back or shouted at a potential landlord like that. But Maja was a badass, just like she said. Maja wasn't going to let anyone push her around. She was kind of like a superhero. The only problem was that if she kept shouting at landlords, they'd never find a place to live.

They got back to the car and Maja turned to Riley. 'Don't ever let anyone push you around or make you feel bad. You be strong, Riley. A strong woman is a great woman.'

Maja had another argument with the landlady of the next apartment and told her that it was only fit for pigs to live in.

Riley was getting really worried by the time they arrived at the third apartment. It was situated halfway between the restaurant and the school, on a small road. It was part of a house that had been divided into three flats. There was a rosebush in the garden and the outside was painted a really pretty shade of blue.

It looked nice. Way nicer than any of the places they'd seen so far. Riley didn't want Maja to fight with this landlord. She crossed her fingers.

They approached the house and Maja rang the bell. A woman opened it and smiled at them.

'You're coming to see the flat?' she asked. Before they could answer, she turned back and shouted something in a different language to a young boy peering out from behind a door.

Maja squeezed Riley's hand and laughed. She began to speak to the landlady in Polish, making the landlady's face light up. They talked and talked, waving their arms around, laughing, rolling their eyes, shaking their heads and laughing some more.

Finally, they stopped talking and the woman showed them upstairs to the flat that was for rent.

It was clean and bright, and although it was very small, it was all painted freshly in white so it seemed bigger. Riley's heart sang. This was perfect. There was no mould on the walls, and the bathroom was spotlessly clean. It was lovely.

Riley watched as Maja negotiated with the landlady. Thankfully Maja wasn't shouting or looking angry; this time she seemed calm. Riley watched and waited nervously for the two women to stop talking. Eventually Maja turned to her. 'You can move in next weekend.'

Riley felt her heart stop. 'Really? Seriously?'

Maja nodded.

'How much is the rent? Is it still eight hundred and fifty?'

Maja winked at her. 'No, it's eight twenty-five. I bargained it down.'

What? Was this for real? Was this actually happening? Were she and Mum going to be able to live in this lovely flat? Riley's heart was fit to burst. She hugged Maja and then the landlady.

'Thank you, thank you, thank you,' she said, and then she burst into tears of relief. Finally, finally they had somewhere to live and it was *nice*. Riley couldn't wait to tell her mum.

Things were finally changing, and for the better. In one week's time they would have a home!

Chapter 17

Mum was still weak on Monday morning, so Maja drove Riley to school. They didn't have to leave early, because Riley could shower and brush her teeth and have breakfast at Maja's. She texted Oleg to tell him she wouldn't be in for breakfast and to tell him the brilliant news about finding a place to live. He was super happy for her.

Before Riley left, Mum said they needed to get out of Maja's hair. 'We mustn't overstay our welcome. She has been so good to us. Giving me a job, finding us an apartment and helping me get better.' Mum said she'd try to sleep a bit more today and then pick Riley up later and they'd go back to sleeping in the car. It would only be for five more nights, so Riley didn't care.

❖

For someone so tough, Maja really loved pop music. She played Taylor Swift's 'Shake It Off' at full volume on the way to school and they both sang loudly as they drove up to the gates. It was kind of hilarious, because Maja thought the song was called 'Take It Off', and that's what she sang the whole time. Riley laughed and sang and felt so happy.

Until she climbed out of the minivan and saw Vanessa coming towards her. Maja sped off, singing 'Take It Off' at the top of her voice.

'Hiiiiiii,' Vanessa said. 'Who was that dropping you to school in a *van*?' She wrinkled her nose.

Riley decided not to lie. 'A good friend.'

'Since when are you friends with a woman covered in tattoos who drives a van?'

Riley needed to be careful here. She didn't want Vanessa knowing any details of her life. 'She works with Mum.'

'Doing what?'

'Lots of stuff.' Riley was deliberately vague.

'Is your Mum hanging out with people like that now?'

'People like what?' Riley challenged. 'Maja is an amazing person, Vanessa.'

'But she looks so … well … *rough*.'

Riley really, really wanted to smack Vanessa in the middle of her nasty, sneering face. Thankfully Sophie arrived behind them just then.

'Hey, guys, how was the weekend?' Sophie asked.

'Good,' Riley said, and for the first time, she meant it.

'Amazing – Mum took me on a shopping spree to the outlet stores. OMG, I got so much new stuff. I'm going to have to throw out half my wardrobe,' Vanessa told them.

'How was yours?' Riley asked Sophie.

'Awful. Because it was raining on Saturday, the boys got bored, which is always a disaster. So they decided it would be a great idea to get the plastic toboggans we got when it snowed last year and go down the stairs and crash into the wall in the hall. They put a mattress up against the wall to stop them from actually killing themselves. But then the twins decided to do it together

151

and they tilted sideways and missed the mattress and Fred broke his arm and Ted broke his leg. Dad was away and Mum said she couldn't trust Tim and Tom to be alone in the house, so we all had to go to the hospital and we spent seven hours waiting for the doctor to put them in plaster.'

'Oh, Sophie, that's awful! Are they OK now?' Riley asked.

'They're fine, and the good news is that Mum has finally agreed that they might all start boarding at their school next year, which is amazing news – for me, anyway.'

'Riley might need to go to boarding school too. You should see the people she's hanging around with,' Vanessa drawled.

Sophie looked confused. 'What?'

'A weird-looking woman with badly dyed red hair, covered in tattoos, just dropped her to school in a van. The kind of person you would be afraid of if they were walking towards you.'

'Who was it?' Sophie asked her best friend.

'Maja. She works with Mum and she is lovely,' Riley said, scowling at Vanessa.

Sophie shrugged. 'Cool. I think some tattoos are kind of nice.'

'Oh my God, they are so disgusting,' said Vanessa, making a face. 'My mum says only people with no education get tattoos, or people who live in flats.'

Riley rolled her eyes. She had always thought Vanessa was a snob, but she'd never realised quite how much of one. She was actually a really nasty person, with an equally nasty mother.

The bell rang and they hurried to class. During history class, Riley whispered to Sophie that she had her birthday present and would give it to her at break-time. 'Let's just go by ourselves to the bench behind the tennis court and I'll give it to you there.' Riley didn't want a crowd when she gave Sophie the gift. She felt bad enough about having stolen the hoodie and she didn't want anyone asking awkward questions, especially not Vanessa. She just wanted to give it to Sophie and get it over with.

'Great!' Sophie squeezed her friend's hand.

They tried to sneak out without Vanessa or anyone following them at break-time, but before they had even reached the end of the corridor, Vanessa shouted at them. 'Wait up!'

Sophie rolled her eyes. They turned around to see Vanessa, Zoe and Grace following them.

Dammit, thought Riley.

'Where are you rushing off to?' Vanessa snapped.

'Riley just wanted to give me my birthday present,' Sophie said.

'In private? Is it a secret or something?' Vanessa turned to Riley.

'No, it's no big deal.' Riley wished they would all just go away.

'So it finally arrived from America,' Zoe said. 'That's good. Sometimes stuff gets lost.'

Riley nodded.

'Well, go on then. Give it to her,' Vanessa snapped.

'I didn't get a chance to wrap it or anything, sorry.'

'Don't be silly, I don't care,' Sophie replied.

Riley reluctantly opened her backpack and pulled out the green sweatshirt. She handed it to Sophie.

'Oh, Riley, I love it. It's gorgeous, thanks so much.' Sophie reached over and hugged her friend.

'I saw those in Hollister on Saturday. You could have got it there and saved all the trouble of getting it from America,' Zoe said.

'Oh, I … I didn't know they had them here. I never saw them.'

'They might only have started selling them in Ireland recently,' Grace noted.

Vanessa pulled the sweatshirt from Sophie's arms. She peered at the tag. 'The price is in euros not dollars. If you did buy it in America, the price would be in dollars.'

Riley felt her face going bright red.

'Who cares about the stupid tag? I love it.' Sophie grabbed the sweatshirt back.

'But why did you say you got it in America if you didn't?' Vanessa was not letting go.

Riley didn't know what to say.

'Why are you so obsessed with where she got it?' Grace asked Vanessa.

Vanessa turned to face her. 'I'm not obsessed with anything. I just don't see why she lied about it.'

'It *is* a bit strange to lie about it,' Zoe agreed.

Riley needed to nip this conversation in the bud before Vanessa started asking any more questions. She tried to think of some excuse, any excuse. 'OK, I did lie about it. I'm sorry, Sophie. Mum has been working weekends and she wasn't able to bring me to get your present. I felt bad about it, so I made up a stupid lie.'

'It's fine, seriously, forget about it. And you didn't need to get me anything, but I love it. I don't care where you got it.'

'Is your mum working every weekend now?' Grace asked.

'Yes.'

'You can come and hang out in my house if you want,' she said. 'It must be boring on your own.'

'Thanks, Grace, but she won't be working so hard anymore.' It was kind of true. Now that they had a place to rent, her mum was going to ask Maja if she could work slightly fewer hours.

'You should have told me she was working every weekend, Riley – you know you can always come to my house,' Sophie said, linking her arm through Riley's.

'Urgh, you should see the people Riley's mother works with. They look like convicts,' Vanessa said. 'My mother would never let me associate with people like that.'

Oleg walked by and bumped his mop handle against the back of Vanessa's head.

'Ouch! Watch where you're going! Are you blind?' she snapped.

Oleg winked at Riley and she grinned.

'He almost knocked me over,' Vanessa huffed.

Pity he didn't, Riley thought.

CHAPTER 18

When Mum picked Riley up from school, she didn't look much better and was coughing a lot.

'Are you OK, Mum?'

'Yes pet, one more good night's sleep and I'll be back to normal.'

Riley crossed her fingers.

When they got back to the restaurant, her mum parked the car.

'I might just have a little lie down,' she said.

Riley helped snuggle her mum up and she fell asleep straight away. Two hours later, she was still asleep.

Maja came out to check on them. 'It's good for Mummy to sleep. Sleep is making her better. Here, I brought you food.' Maja handed Riley a bowl of stew, which she ate greedily. She was starving.

Maja produced a second bowl. 'When Mummy wakes up, you give her this soup. Very good soup. It will help her with energy.'

'Thank you, Maja,' Riley said.

'You stay with Mummy and make sure she is taking tablets when she wakes up.'

'I will.'

'You get results of Friday test?'

'Yes.'

'Did you do good?'

'Better than last week.'

Maja smiled. 'Good. This week better again and so on. Soon, you will be genius like Albert Einstein.'

Riley giggled. 'I don't think so.'

Maja smiled. 'Riley, you can be anything – you just have to go to school and work hard. You can be three-shock one day.'

'Three-shock?' Riley didn't understand.

'Yes, three-shock, leader of Ireland.'

'Oh … *Taoiseach*,' Riley grinned.

'That's what I said. Three-shock. Irish is complicated language. Crazy words that make crazy sounds. I am good at languages, but Irish is too hard.'

'I agree,' Riley said. She struggled with Irish too. It was super-complicated, but everyone had to learn it in school.

'You will be Three-shock one day and make all landlords be nice to people or else they go to prison.'

Riley giggled. 'OK, I will.' She would make Maja, Oleg and Mum ministers, she said.

Maja grinned. 'See, I give you good ideas. You also make me Irish citizen.'

'Of course.'

They laughed. Maja took Riley's empty bowl and turned to go back into the restaurant.

'Maja?'

'Yes?'

'If you had a friend who was nasty and mean, what would you do?'

'I would slap her in face and never speak to her again.'

Riley smiled. 'What if you couldn't slap her, because then you'd get into trouble?'

'I would slap her when no one is looking.'

Riley laughed.

Maja paused. 'Look, Riley, some people make your life better. Some people make your life bad. You walk away from bad people. They poison your life. You only stay friends with good people.' She looked at her watch and cursed. 'I have to go now. If you need me, come find me.'

Riley lay back down beside her mum. The problem was that if she walked away from Vanessa, she was also walking away from Sophie. Sophie was stuck with Vanessa because they were cousins. So Riley was stuck with her too. Next year when they went into secondary school, it would be fresh start. Maybe then Riley could get away from Vanessa. She hoped so. As Maja said, she was poison.

Riley was awake most of the night because of her mum's coughing. She slept, coughed, slept and coughed.

At five in the morning, Riley gave up, sat up in the car and took out her book. Her mum coughed and woke up.

Riley wiped her mum's hot forehead with a facecloth that she had poured bottled water onto.

'Thank you, darling,' Mum croaked. 'That feels lovely.'

'Do you feel any better?' Riley asked. She was praying her mum did feel better, but she knew by looking at her that she didn't.

'Yes, a little.'

'Mum, I think you should go to the doctor.'

'No, pet, I'm fine. Doctors are expensive. This is just a temperature and a cough. It'll go soon. I need to get back to work today. We need the money for the new apartment.'

Riley looked at her mother. She had barely eaten in four days. She looked even tinier than before. There was no way she could work, but they did need the money. Riley felt her chest tighten. If Mum couldn't work, they wouldn't be able to pay next month's rent. They'd get kicked out of the lovely apartment. *Please, God, make her better. Please*, Riley begged. They couldn't lose the apartment – they needed it. They needed a place to live. Riley couldn't live in the car much longer. It was killing her. She was so tired from not sleeping properly. So tired from being afraid of every sound at night. Afraid of being robbed, attacked or beaten up.

She was sick of washing her hair in the restaurant sink on Sundays, washing her clothes in the sink, not having a shower, not having a bed, not having a home. Riley really wanted a home. Somewhere she could go and close the door and be safe and clean and eat sitting on a chair at a table and sleep in an actual bed.

All the things Riley had taken for granted, she now missed so much. They couldn't live like this anymore. Mum had to get better.

Riley sat opposite Oleg, eating her cornflakes.

'You're quiet today. What's going on in that head?'

'Mum's still sick. I'm scared she'll lose her job. Maja is really nice but she's not going to pay Mum for not working. I want her to go to the doctor. She said it's too expensive. But what if she gets sicker, Oleg? I can't lose my mum too.' Riley dropped her spoon into the bowl and began to cry.

'Hey now. Your mum will be fine. She's probably just exhausted from working and worrying. The body needs rest. Here's what we'll do. If she isn't any better tomorrow, call me and I'll bring you both to my doctor.'

'But we can't pay for it.'

'Don't worry, Riley, I'll sort it out. Your mum can pay me when she gets back on her feet.'

Riley held back tears of gratitude. 'Thank you so much. Maybe she just needs a prescription for stronger medicine?'

Oleg nodded. 'Yes, maybe she needs antibiotics.'

Riley immediately felt better. They had a plan now and the doctor would make Mum better. Her chest felt a little bit less tight.

'Thanks, Oleg.'

'No problem.'

'Also,' she said, grinning, 'thanks for accidentally on purpose bumping into Vanessa yesterday.'

He smiled. 'I don't know what you're talking about.'

Oleg's phone pinged. A photo of a boy wearing a party hat, sitting in front of a birthday cake, came up on the screen.

'Is that your little boy?' Riley asked.

Oleg nodded. 'He is nine today,' he said quietly.

'Oh, Oleg, you're missing his birthday. Here's me going on about my problems. I'm so sorry. It must be so hard for you.'

Oleg shrugged. 'Days like this are difficult. But I am doing this for him, so he can have a better education and a better life. I have to keep reminding myself of that.'

'You're an amazing dad. He's a lucky boy,' Riley said, tears filling her eyes.

So many people's lives were so hard. She'd never realised it before. But so many people were struggling to survive or make better lives for their families. She had lived in her own bubble, in her big house with wardrobes filled with clothes and a fridge stuffed full of food. But that wasn't the way most people lived.

The world was a very different place to the way Riley had thought it was.

CHAPTER 19

Mum gasped for air in between coughing fits. Riley was terrified. She rubbed her mother's back but the coughing was getting worse. It was three in the morning and Riley didn't know what to do.

Mum couldn't speak because she was either coughing or trying to breathe. Riley began to panic. What could she do?

Eventually she decided to call Oleg. She dialled his number and prayed he'd answer. He did.

Riley sobbed down the phone. 'Mum can't breathe. It's bad, Oleg, really bad.'

'OK, tell me where you are. I'm coming now.'

Riley gave him the address of the restaurant and explained that they were parked in the little car park at the side of the restaurant. Then she pulled on her shoes and a hoodie and unlocked the iron gate.

Her mum continued to gasp for breath as Riley prayed to God and cried. Ten minutes later, Oleg came hurtling around the corner in his van. Riley jumped out of the car and ran around to open the boot.

Oleg took one look at Mum and turned to Riley. 'You did the right thing. She needs to go to hospital now.'

He picked Mum up and carried her to his van.

'Who are you?' Mum croaked.

'He's my friend from school,' Riley explained.

'What?' Mum looked confused.

'It's OK,' said Oleg. 'I work at Riley's school. I'm the caretaker.'

'I remember you now. You're the kind man who gives Riley breakfast,' Mum said, before her eyes closed and she fell asleep again.

167

Oleg drove as fast as he could to the closest hospital. He parked the van outside the main doors and carried Mum into the A&E department.

He rushed up to the desk with Riley hot on his heels.

'We need urgent help. She's having trouble breathing.'

The nurse ordered a wheelchair for Mum and said they'd have her checked out as soon as possible. Oleg carried her over to the wheelchair, then went to move his van.

'We need to take some details. Is this your mum?' the nurse asked Riley.

She nodded.

'What's her name?'

'Alison Hannigan.'

'Address?'

'I … we … don't have an address right now. We're between homes.'

The nurse frowned. 'Where are you living at the moment?'

Riley looked down, ashamed. 'In our car.'

'Oh …' the nurse said. 'I'm sorry.'

'Please make my mum better,' Riley sobbed. 'She's all I have.'

The nurse reached out and took Riley's hand. 'We'll do everything we can to help her. Don't you worry.'

The nurse disappeared. A few minutes later she came back through the big swing doors. 'They'll see you now,' she said.

Oleg had returned from parking the van by now, so he wheeled Mum into the cubicle, with Riley following close behind. A nurse helped lift Mum onto the bed and propped her up with pillows.

Then they did tests, lots of tests, and X-rays, and finally they put an oxygen mask over Mum's face to help her breathe. Doctors came and went. Nurses came and went. Eventually, four hours later, a doctor came and sat on the bed beside Mum, who was fast asleep.

'My name is Doctor Keane. Is this lady your wife?' she asked Oleg.

'No, I am a friend. This is Riley, Alison's daughter.'

'Oh, OK. Well, Riley, your mum has bacterial pneumonia.'

Riley gasped. She knew that was bad. 'Please don't let her die.'

'Don't worry. We are going to give her antibiotics and oxygen to help her breathe and she will feel better soon. Your mum is going to be fine.'

'Really?'

'Yes.'

'Promise?'

'I promise. But she needs a lot of rest and some strong antibiotics to get her back on her feet. Now I have to see some other patients, but I'll be back to check on your mum very soon.'

'Thank you,' Riley whispered. Her voice broke and when the doctor left, she bent her head over her mother's legs and sobbed.

Oleg patted her on the back. 'There, there, it's all going to be fine. Your mum is in the right place, getting the best care.'

But what about her work? What about the apartment? What about the future? Mum was too weak to work in the restaurant. What were they going to do? Riley was so scared and tired. Eventually she cried herself to sleep.

She woke up sitting in a chair by her mother's bed, with her head resting on a pillow and a blanket covering her.

She was exhausted from the long, dark night.

She looked around. Oleg was gone. She checked her phone. He'd left her a message. 'Had to go to work. Call when you wake up. Your mum will be fine. Don't worry.'

Riley rubbed her eyes. It was ten o'clock. She looked at her mum. She was sleeping and her breathing sounded better – it wasn't all raggedy anymore. She looked more peaceful.

As Riley was about to text Oleg back, a nurse came to say they were moving her mum up to a hospital ward on the third floor. The nurse and a porter helped push the bed into the lift and took her up to the ward.

They put Mum in the far corner. 'This is the best spot,' the nurse whispered, 'beside the window. She can look out at the trees and the sky.'

'Thank you,' Riley said.

'Are you hungry, pet? I can get you some tea and toast.'

Riley realised that she was starving. 'Are you sure that's OK?'

'Of course.'

'That would be amazing.'

The nurse checked Mum's temperature and blood pressure. 'Good news: her temperature is coming down already.' She smiled at Riley. 'I'll be back with some toast for you.'

Riley went to the bathroom and washed her face. When she got back, Mum was awake.

'Where am I?' Mum was confused.

'You're in hospital, Mum. You got really bad last night – you have pneumonia. But they said you're going to be fine.'

'Oh, Riley, I'm so sorry. You must have got such a fright.' Mum began to cry. 'I'm so, so sorry.'

'It's OK, Mum, please don't cry.'

But she was sobbing. 'You deserve more. You deserve a good life. You're such a wonderful girl. You shouldn't be looking after me, I should be looking after you.'

Riley held her mum's hand and they cried and cried. They cried for their old life, they cried from exhaustion, from sadness, from worry and from fear of the future.

They cried because they didn't know what was going to happen next.

CHAPTER 20

Riley was reading her book in the chair beside her mum's bed. Mum was fast asleep when a woman popped her head around the curtain that separated Mum from the patient in the next bed.

'Hello, you must be Riley,' the lady said, smiling.

'Yes.'

'I'm Doreen, and I work here in the hospital.'

'Hello …' Riley wasn't sure what this was about.

'What age are you, Riley?'

'I'm twelve.'

'And this is your mum, Alison?'

'Yes.'

'Is your dad around?'

'No, he died last year.'

'Oh, I'm very sorry to hear that. So the man who brought your mum in, is he a friend?'

'Yes, he's a very good friend.'

'Does he live with you?'

'Oh no, he has his own family.'

'And did I hear you are living in your car? Is that right?'

Riley wriggled in the chair. She didn't like all these questions and Doreen was writing down lots of notes.

'We are, but only for a few more days. We have an apartment that we are moving into this weekend.'

'I see. How long have you been living in your car?'

'Not long.'

'How long?'

'Just a couple of weeks.' Riley tried to be vague.

'Are you going to school?'

'Yes.'

'Are you able to concentrate?'

'Well, not as much as usual, but it'll all be fine after this weekend when we move into our new place and Mum is well again and able to work.'

'What does your mum do?'

'She works in a restaurant.'

'Do you have any uncles, aunts or other family close by?'

'No, just my Uncle Martin, but he's in rehab.'

Doreen scribbled down more notes. 'Are you getting enough to eat?'

'Yes.' Riley decided not to tell her about breakfast with Oleg. She had a feeling it was best not to say too much.

'Do any of your teachers or friends know you're homeless?'

'No, we didn't want anyone to know. And besides, we aren't homeless anymore.'

Doreen stopped writing and looked at Riley. 'The thing is, Riley, your mum won't be able to work for a while. I'm not sure she's in a position to look after you properly. We need to look at what's best for you. We might need to place you elsewhere for a little while.'

'What?' Riley was shocked. Place her elsewhere –
what did that mean? Separate her from Mum? She
looked down at her lap so that Doreen wouldn't see her
welling up.

'Who are you?'

Riley looked up to see her Polish superhero standing
behind Doreen, who jumped with fright at the woman's
sudden appearance.

'Why are you telling Riley her mummy is not looking
after her properly?'

'I'm the hospital social worker. Who are you?'

Maja's eyes narrowed. 'I am friend. And I don't like
you people. So nosy. Always looking into other people's
business.' Maja grabbed Riley's hand and pulled her
out of the ward.

Doreen rushed after them. 'The wellbeing of this
child is my priority here!'

'Wellbeing, my ass,' Maja huffed. 'Riley needs to be
with her mummy.'

'Her mother is not able to look after her. She is living
in her car,' Doreen snapped back.

'Not living in car – this weekend they are moving
into nice apartment.'

'How is her mother going to pay the rent if she can't work? How is she going to look after her child while she recovers from pneumonia?'

'Riley is a big girl. She is able to look after herself while Alison gets better.'

'Riley is a twelve-year-old child,' Doreen reminded Maja. 'She needs adult care.'

'When I was twelve I looked after myself. Riley is strong and I am helping. I know you people – you want to put her into a children's home. I was in a home in Poland, and it was not good place. It was bad place.'

A home? Like a care home? A foster home for kids with no parents? Riley's heart thumped in her chest. Was Doreen going to take her away from her mum? Was she trying to say Alison was a bad mother?

'No no no no!' she said. 'I'm not leaving Mum. She's a great mother. So loving and kind and … and she's my whole world.' Riley began to cry.

Maja put her hand on Riley's shoulder and squeezed. 'Nobody is taking you anywhere.'

'What is your relationship to this child?' Doreen asked.

Maja poked Doreen in the chest. 'You are not asking me questions, Missus. I am not answering you.'

'Don't let her take me away from Mum,' Riley sobbed.

'Riley, I'm here to help you, to keep you safe while your mum gets better,' Doreen explained.

'Hi, Riley, what's going on?'

Riley looked up to see Oleg walking towards her holding a bunch of red tulips. She ran to him and he put an arm around her.

'This social worker is saying Mum is a bad mother and Maja says they're going to try to put me in a home or something.'

Doreen shook her head. 'I didn't say your mum is a bad mother, just that she isn't capable of looking after you while she's unwell.'

Oleg patted Riley on the back. 'Now, now, don't worry, we'll sort this all out.' He shook Maja's hand. 'I've heard a lot about you.'

'Oh yes, and who are you?'

'This is Oleg – he's my friend. He works in my school and looks after me and gives me breakfast every day.'

Maja smiled at him. 'You are a good man.'

'Excuse me, but did Riley say you work at her school?' Doreen was furiously writing notes again.

Oleg and Maja looked at each other. Riley saw them very slightly nod at each other. They understood something that she didn't.

'Yes. I'm the caretaker there and I occasionally give Riley some breakfast if she's been too busy to get some. But her mother looks after her very well.'

'Yes, Alison is very good mother,' Maja agreed.

Doreen continued to scribble notes. 'Riley, how often do you go to school with no breakfast?' she asked gently.

'You say nothing,' Maja said to Riley. Turning to Doreen, she said, 'You lady, you go. Go now. Go … go … go!' Maja roared and shooed Doreen away.

'I'll be back later to talk to you, Riley. It's my job to keep you safe,' Doreen said as she backed away down the corridor.

Riley looked at Maja and Oleg. They were both frowning.

'This is bad,' Maja said.

'Yes, we need to do something quickly to stop Riley entering into the system.'

Riley's head was pounding. 'Please, please don't let them take me away from Mum,' she pleaded.

Oleg patted her shoulder. 'No one is taking you away from your mum, don't worry.'

'I will deal with Doreen, don't you worry,' Maja added.

But Riley *was* worried – very, very worried. Worried down to the tips of her toes.

CHAPTER 21

Oleg, Maja and Riley went to the café opposite the hospital. Riley sipped a hot chocolate. The lump in her throat would only allow her to swallow tiny sips.

Maja and Oleg stood outside on the footpath talking. Maja was waving her arms and Oleg kept shaking his head. They seemed to be arguing about something, but then they both nodded and shook hands.

They came back into the café and sat down beside Riley.

'OK, Riley, Maja and I have been talking and trying to work out a solution to the current problem,' Oleg said gently.

'Social worker will not let go now,' Maja explained. 'Your mummy is too sick to look after you or work for me. You need help, and Oleg has found solution.'

Oleg turned to Riley. 'You told me that your mother hadn't spoken to her parents since she dropped out of college and married your dad, but they are probably still alive, yes?'

'I guess so. I don't know. Mum never talks about them.'

'What was your mum's surname before she got married?' Oleg asked.

'Murphy.'

Oleg groaned. 'The most common name in the country. Do you know where they live?'

'Mum grew up in a small town outside Galway. It's called Rockstone.' Mum had only mentioned it once or twice, but Riley remembered it because it made her think of 'rockstar'.

Oleg smiled. 'OK, good, that will help narrow it down. Do you have any idea what your grandparents did?'

'You mean as jobs?' Riley tried to think back to the very, very few times her mum had ever mentioned her parents. 'I don't know what my grandad does, but I know my grandmother is a doctor. Mum said she used to spend Saturdays stuck in the surgery reading books while her mum saw patients.'

'OK, good. Do you know what her name is?'

Riley smiled. 'Yes, it's Florence.'

Riley knew this because she remembered talking to her mum about names and her mum saying that Riley was lucky to have a nice name, and that some people called their daughters after their grandmothers. 'I certainly wasn't going to name you after my mother or your dad's mother,' Mum had laughed. 'Besides, as soon as I saw you, I just knew you could never be a Betty or a Florence.'

Riley was pleased she'd remembered all this information.

'Good girl, now we know a lot about Granny,' Maja said.

'But why do you want to know about her? She was horrible to Mum. She's a bad person. So is my grandad.'

Oleg and Maja looked at each other. 'Riley,' Oleg said gently, 'we have to find a relative to help you and your mum. What happened was a long time ago. I'm sure they have forgiven her and would love to meet you.'

Riley pushed her hot chocolate away, 'No. No way. They are bad people who treated my mum like dirt. I'm not going to live with them. No way. Are you crazy? I'll look after Mum – I can do it. Maja, you said you did it, you looked after yourself, and you said I was strong.'

Maja's eyes filled with tears. Riley was shocked – she had never seen Maja upset.

'Riley, I did look after myself, but it was not good. I am strong but I had bad childhood. I want you to have good one. You are smart girl. You need to stay in school and have great life.'

'But my grandparents won't want to look after me and Mum – they hate Mum.'

Oleg put his hand on her arm. 'No parent hates their child. They were angry and upset, but it was a long time ago, and I am sure they miss your mum and will be so happy to know they have a wonderful granddaughter.'

Riley shook her head. 'No. I won't ask them for help. Mum would hate it. She'd rather live in the car. If she wanted them to help, she would have asked them.'

Oleg's voice was firm. 'Riley, you and your mum need help. Your mum is very weak. It could be a long time before she gets better. She can't go back to the car. She needs an adult to look after her. It's not your job to be the grown up – you need to be a kid and go to school and not worry about your mum.'

'But I can do it! I'll stay off school until Mum is better.'

Maja slapped the table. 'Riley, you are great kid but you need help! If you don't find your grandparents, social worker will put you in a home until Mummy gets better – and maybe for ever.'

'What?' Riley burst into tears.

'For goodness' sake, how is that helpful?' Oleg glared at Maja.

'She needs to know the situation is very serious.' Maja glared right back at him.

'We don't know anything for sure.' Oleg kept his voice very calm. 'But Doreen does now know that you are living in your car and that your mum is too sick to look after you. We have to find your grandparents.'

'But what if they don't want to help?' Riley asked.

'They will,' Oleg said. 'They are your mum's parents, and she's a lovely person. So I'm sure they are nice too.'

'I will make them help,' Maja growled.

Riley looked at Oleg's and Maja's serious faces. She knew she had no choice. She'd have to find her grandparents, who she didn't know and who had been so horrible to her mum, and beg them for help.

CHAPTER 22

Riley sat in the back of Oleg's van, with Maja up front. They had googled 'Dr Florence Murphy, Rockstone, Galway', and thankfully only one had come up. Riley stared at the profile photo of her grandmother. She looked so like Riley's mum, it was freaky. Same height, same blue eyes, same button nose. It was like looking at an older version of her mum.

They'd set off at five in the morning. They wanted to be outside Florence's surgery when it opened at eight o'clock. Riley could feel the tension in the van. Maja kept telling Oleg he was going the wrong way and Oleg kept telling Maja to stop being a back-seat driver.

'I am not in back seat,' Maja said. 'Riley is in back seat.'

'It's an expression, Maja, it means stop telling me how to drive.'

'I am helping you get there quicker.'

'I know how to get to Galway, thank you.'

'Pffff, men. Men never want help. Always know best. Never wrong. That's why I never marry. No man is telling me what to do. No man is telling me I'm wrong.'

Oleg laughed. 'I think most men would be terrified to tell you you're wrong about anything, Maja.'

Maja winked at Riley in the mirror. 'See, I am the boss, Riley!'

Riley tried to laugh along, but she was too nervous. She held Tiger tightly to her chest. She knew she was getting too old for cuddly toys, but she needed his furry comfort now. She'd lied to Mum and told her she was in school. She'd lied to school and told them she was at home with her mum. And now, here she was on her way to Galway to ask for help from her grandparents, who were complete strangers, with her two new friends – Oleg and Maja.

It was so strange that this man and woman were now the most important people in Riley's life after Mum. They had literally saved Mum's life. Riley's heart was full of love and gratitude that they had come into her life. She would be completely lost without them.

'You have kids, Oleg?' Maja asked.

'Yes, two. Do you?' Oleg asked.

Maja shook her head. 'No kids for me. I am too busy for kids. I looked after my little brothers and sisters when I was young. They drove me crazy. I do not want kids now. I want to live my life without worrying about kids. I had enough worry when I was young. Now is time for no worries. Now is time for freedom.' Maja waved her hands in the air.

Oleg laughed. 'I can see that you are a very independent woman.'

'Yes, I am. I think you are a good daddy,' Maja said to Oleg. 'You are kind man. This is important. My father was not kind man.'

'Thanks – and I'm sorry your father was not kind.'

Maja shrugged. 'Having bad father made me strong. Out of bad comes good, I think.'

Riley hoped Maja was right. But she wasn't sure she believed it. Riley thought that out of bad came more bad. Dad had died, they'd lost all their money, Mum had got sick and now Riley was going to have to beg her mean grandparents to help her. Where was the good in any of that?

Oleg caught Riley's eye in the mirror. 'What about you, Riley? Would you like to have kids when you're older?'

Riley looked out of the window at the grey sky. Would she like to have kids?

When she saw the way her mum looked at her, with so much love, she knew she'd like to have that for her own child. Love was very powerful. When Mum looked at her, she could feel her mother's love warming up her heart. Yes, Riley would like to have that with her own child one day. But only if she had the money to look after them, a house that she owned that couldn't be taken away from her and a good job. Riley would never, ever, want her child to experience living in a car or being cold and hungry and scared all the time. It was too hard. Riley felt so tired, tired down in her bones.

'I don't know,' was what she said to Oleg.

'No kids until you are thirty. University and good job first,' Maja told Riley.

Despite her nerves, Riley drifted into sleep as she listened to Maja and Oleg chatting about their countries and arguing over whether Polish or Moldovan food was better.

Riley was dreaming about bubble baths. She was lying in a warm bath full of bubbles that smelled of strawberries. She felt so cosy and clean.

'Riley … Riley …' She felt someone shaking her gently.

Riley didn't want to wake up. This was a lovely dream. She slowly opened her eyes and looked around. They were parked in an empty car park, outside a building with a big sign that said 'GP Clinic'.

Riley was wide awake within seconds. They were here. This was where her grandmother worked. She looked at her watch. It was a quarter to eight; her grandmother would be here any minute. Riley's heart raced.

She climbed out of the car and stretched with Maja and Oleg. The sound of an engine caught their attention. The three of them turned to see a silver car pulling into the car park.

Riley's heart stopped.

CHAPTER 23

A well-dressed woman stepped out of the silver car. She was the same woman Riley had seen in the photo online. She was wearing smart black trousers, a white shirt with a black bow on the front and a black raincoat.

Riley hid behind Oleg and Maja, peeping out to look at her grandmother.

'She doesn't look like monster,' Maja whispered.

'She looks nice,' Oleg said.

Riley said nothing. Her head was spinning. This was her *actual* grandmother.

The woman pulled a big bag out of the back of her car. When she turned to lock it, she noticed the little group staring at her.

She raised her hand and smiled at them. 'Morning! Are you my first patients? Come on in.'

She unlocked the clinic door and held it open for them. Riley kept her head down as she hurried past her grandmother.

Florence switched on the lights and asked them to give her a minute to get her room ready. 'My receptionist will be in at eight, but I can see you now and get an early start.'

While they waited in reception for her to call them in, Riley thought she might faint. She looked around the waiting room. It was very neat and tidy. The magazines were fanned out perfectly. There were three big leafy potted plants and a water cooler. There were three names on the board behind reception: Dr Florence Murphy, Dr Greg Haddington and Dr Rosemary Byrne.

The door swung open and a man walked in.

'Hello, are you waiting for me? Dr Haddington?' he asked.

'No, for Dr Murphy,' Oleg answered.

'Well, you're in good hands. She's the best.' He smiled at them and went to his room.

Florence popped her head out and called them in. Maja went first, then Oleg and finally Riley. Oleg squeezed Riley's hand.

They sat down opposite Florence, who was sitting sideways behind her desk, typing into her computer.

'Now, which one of you is the patient?' she asked, turning to look at Maja.

'We are not sick. We are having a problem,' Maja said.

'We're not here for medical advice, exactly,' Oleg explained.

Florence frowned. 'I don't understand.'

'We are here because of Riley,' Oleg said.

Florence's eyes turned to focus on Riley. Riley raised her face and stared right at her grandmother. *Yes, here I am, Granny. Here is your granddaughter, the one you didn't even know existed. The child of the woman you banished. Have a good look at me.*

Florence stared and stared. Riley stared right back.

Florence's hands gripped the edge of her desk. 'I don't … what … I …'

Riley sat completely still, unable to move, staring straight into her grandmother's eyes.

'Are … is …?' Florence stumbled over her words.

'Riley is your granddaughter,' Oleg said quietly.

Florence jumped back in her chair. '*What?*'

'Her mummy is Alison, your daughter,' Maja said.

'Alison? Oh my goodness. Oh … oh …' Florence was gasping for air.

Oleg rushed out to get her a glass of water.

Riley still didn't move.

'Riley is a fantastic girl. You will be so proud.' Maja patted Riley on the back.

Oleg returned and handed Florence the water. She drank some and placed the cup down with trembling hands.

'I didn't know … I never heard. Oh, you do look so like Ali.'

Ali. The only other person who called her mum Ali had been her dad. Riley said nothing.

'Where is Alison? Is she OK? She's not … Oh God.' Florence covered her mouth with her hand.

'Relax, Granny, she's not dead,' Maja said.

'Alison is fine,' Oleg explained calmly. 'Well, she's in hospital with pneumonia but she's going to be fine.'

'Oh, thank God.' Florence's voice was shaking.

Riley glared at her. Why was she pretending to care about her daughter now? She'd kicked her out years ago and never contacted her since. She'd banished her only child from her life. 'You left her all alone and never spoke to her and now suddenly you care? How could you do that? What kind of person are you?' Riley cried out.

Florence's face fell. 'I did try to contact her, but she never replied. I suppose she was angry. We were wrong.' Florence began to get emotional. 'We were wrong to push her away. My husband was so angry – he was heartbroken that Alison had given everything up for Frank. He didn't think he was … well … they didn't get on.'

'My dad was a good man. He loved me and Mum so much,' Riley said. 'But he's dead now, so that should make you happy.' Suddenly, all of the anger and rage that Riley felt about everything that had happened to her and her mum boiled over. 'He died of a heart attack nearly six months ago. He lost all of his money. We were kicked out of our house and we have been living in the back of our car. My mum, *your daughter*, is really sick because she was working so hard to try to get us a place to live. But you don't care. You horrible, selfish woman! You left her. You abandoned her. You broke her heart. She never talked about you because if she ever did she'd just cry. Mum would never hurt anyone – she is so kind. I don't know how she can be your daughter. You are a cruel person.'

Florence looked at Maja and Oleg in utter disbelief. They nodded.

'Living in your car? Oh God, I'm so sorry. I'm sorry about your dad, I'm sorry about Alison, I'm sorry about *everything.*'

Riley stood up and leaned across the desk. 'It's not good enough. Saying sorry doesn't take away all of Mum's pain. Saying sorry doesn't make up for hurting Mum, the sweetest person in the world. How could you do that to her? How could you do that to *us?*' Riley sobbed. Oleg gently pulled her back into her chair and handed her a tissue. He put a comforting arm around her shoulder.

Florence cleared her throat and gathered herself together. 'Riley, I am incredibly sorry for all you have been through. I did try to get in touch with Alison. I tried many times. But the only address I had was your dad's head office. Ali changed her phone and you moved house. I rang but Frank refused to give me her new number. I wrote to her at your dad's shop but I don't think he gave her the letters. I drove up to the shop and begged him to tell her to call me, but he was angry. Angry that we didn't like him and angry that we wouldn't invest in his business.'

Riley said nothing. That did sound like her dad. He had been obsessed with his business and was always asking people to invest in it, even Riley's friends' dads. Mum had hated when he'd done that. She was embarrassed that he was asking people he didn't really know for money. But that was Dad: he was always doing deals, and he never switched off.

'If you really want to find someone you can find them,' Maja said.

Florence nodded. 'I know. But when I realised how much Frank hated us and how much he wanted us out of Ali's life, I knew that if I forced her to see me it would cause problems in her marriage. So I left it. She knew where we lived, and she knew where I worked. All she had to do was call.'

'But she didn't know you had looked for her,' Riley said. 'She told me you never contacted her again.'

Tears ran down Florence's face. 'I know you may not believe it, but I adored her. She was our only child, and we loved her so much. We had such high hopes for her. She was going to be a successful lawyer and travel the world. But then she met your dad and he said university was a waste of time and she dropped out and gave up her whole life for him.'

'She loved him,' Riley said.

'Oh, I know she did. She adored him,' Florence agreed.

'He was a good dad – he was just bad at business and money and stuff.'

'I'm glad he was a good father to you.'

Maja clapped her hands. 'OK, now we know you love Alison and you are not bad woman, we need to talk about fixing the problem.'

'I'll do anything to help,' Florence said.

Oleg leant forward. 'Alison is going to need a few weeks to recover fully. So she can't look after Riley. The social workers are moving in: they've found out that Alison and Riley have been living in their car. If we can't find a family member to help, they may be separated.'

Florence jumped up. 'No one is going to separate my family again. Ever.'

'Good, Granny, good! You make up for all the years you were a bad granny,' Maja cheered.

'Mum won't let you look after us. She hates you,' Riley reminded Florence.

Florence's shoulders slumped.

Oleg took Riley's hand. 'Riley, there seems to be a lot your mum doesn't know about. Why don't we let Florence come and talk to her?'

'I don't want Mum to be upset and get sicker.'

Florence came around and stood in front of Riley. 'I promise I won't upset her. All I want to do is help. Please let me talk to her. If she asks me to leave, I will.'

'What about Grandad?' Riley asked. 'I bet you he won't want to help.'

Florence looked away. 'Nigel died three years ago.'

'Oh.' Riley didn't know what to say.

'Sorry to hear that,' Oleg said.

'It's better, only Granny and Alison and Riley are making decisions now. Women are good at solving problems,' Maja said.

'If you'll let me, I'd love to help you and get to know you,' Florence said softly to Riley.

'I don't know. Only if Mum says it's OK,' Riley said.

'Absolutely,' Florence agreed.

'Riley is one in a million,' Oleg said.

'She is incredible girl, and you are lucky granny,' Maja added.

Florence nodded. 'You are lucky to have such good friends,' she said to Riley.

'I know,' Riley said, slipping her hands into Maja's and Oleg's.

The little group headed out. Florence told the receptionist to cancel all her appointments for the rest of the week.

'Is everything OK, Doctor Murphy?' she asked.

Florence looked at Riley. 'Yes. My family needs me, and I need to be there for them.'

They walked out into the car park and headed back to Dublin for the big reunion.

CHAPTER 24

Riley looked out at the fields whizzing by. What was her mum going to say when Florence walked into the hospital room? Riley was worried that her mum would be furious. Would she think Riley had betrayed her by running to find Florence?

But then Florence had said she'd tried to contact Alison but Dad had blocked her. Riley felt a bit sick about that. He shouldn't have done that.

Riley loved her dad, but he had made a lot of mistakes, borrowing money from everyone and not telling Mum her parents wanted to see her. She was realising that grown-ups made a lot of mistakes. Life was so much more complicated than Riley had ever imagined.

Maja leaned back and handed Riley a croissant that she had got from the garage while Oleg filled the car with petrol. But Riley couldn't eat; she was too nervous.

'You need to eat,' Maja said.

'I'll eat after Mum sees Florence,' Riley replied.

'Hold it and maybe you will have a few bites. Try, Riley. You need energy.'

'She's right,' Oleg said. 'You do need to eat something. This has been a very emotional day.'

And it's only just begun, Riley thought.

'Wow, a man says I am right. You hear that, Riley? This is miracle. Men never say women are right, always we are wrong. Oleg is a good man.'

Oleg laughed and shook his head. 'Some men are good, Maja – in fact lots of men are.'

'Lots no, some yes,' Maja agreed. 'So, Riley, your granny is not so bad.'

'I guess.'

'She tried to contact your mummy but your stupid

daddy said no. Sorry to call your daddy stupid, but he was.'

'Well, I'm sure he thought he was doing the right thing.' Riley tried to defend her father.

'What right thing? Keeping granny from daughter and granddaughter? How is this right thing?' Maja snapped.

'We don't know the full story so we shouldn't judge,' Oleg said.

'I judge. I see a stupid thing, I say so.'

'Sometimes, Maja, you don't have to say every single thing that you are thinking. Sometimes you need to consider other people's feelings,' Oleg told her.

Maja crossed her arms. 'No. I say like I see. I tell the truth. Good is good, stupid is stupid.'

Riley closed her eyes and pretended to sleep to block out the constant back and forth between Oleg and Maja. She was so grateful to them both, but they were exhausting.

When they arrived at the hospital car park, Florence followed them in through the main doors. Riley peeped up at her. Florence's eyes were red and puffy from crying. *Good,* Riley thought, *she has a heart and she is sorry.*

When they reached the third floor, Florence walked straight over to the nurses' station. Riley watched her grandmother, in a very polite but firm voice, insist on speaking to the nurse in charge. She spoke to her about Mum and got an update on her health.

Then Florence came back over to them. 'Her temperature has stabilised and her breathing is much better. She's still weak but much improved, which is great news.'

'OK, now we go in. I have to be in restaurant in one hour. I stay to make sure you are nice to Alison and Riley, then I will go,' Maja said.

Oleg turned to Riley. 'I think you should go in and talk to your mum first. Prepare her for meeting Florence again.'

'I'm scared she's going to be angry.' Riley's lip trembled.

Oleg looked into her eyes. 'You have nothing to be afraid of. We are all here for you. Just tell your mum the truth. Tell her about the social worker and how much Florence wants to see her and help her.'

Riley nervously walked into the ward and over to her mum's bed. She was sitting up, looking very pale, but much better. 'Hello, darling,' she said, putting her arms out, and Riley hugged her tight. 'I'm sorry I gave you a fright. I'm much better and the doctor says I can get out in a few days. I'll get straight back to work to pay for the apartment. Don't worry, I'll sort it out.' Mum bent over and coughed painfully.

'Mum, I've got something to tell you,' Riley said, her voice shaking.

'What is it? Oh, Riley, what's happened?'

Through tears and hiccups, Riley told her mum about the last twenty-four hours. She told her about Doreen, the social worker who knew they were living in their car, about how Oleg and Maja had said she had to get help and then, finally, about finding Florence.

'*What?*' Mum's eyes widened in shock. 'You found my mother? How?'

Riley told her about Maja and Oleg helping.

Mum cried and held Riley close. 'I am so sorry. I am so sorry you've had all this worry and stress. I will make this up to you, somehow. I will find a way.'

Riley pulled back. 'Mum, you have to talk to Granny. I don't want us to be split up. She did try to contact you lots of times, but Dad wouldn't let her. She'll tell you herself, but she's not so bad and she loves you.'

It was Mum's turn to bury her head in her hands and sob.

'Please, Mum, we need help,' Riley begged.

Mum nodded, unable to speak. Riley gently placed Tiger in the bed beside her mum to give her strength and comfort.

Then she went out and told Florence to come in.

Florence came and stood by the side of the bed. Mum pulled her hands slowly down from her eyes.

'Oh, Ali,' Florence said, tears running down her face. 'Oh, my poor Ali. I'm so sorry, pet.'

Riley left them alone. From the side of the room, Oleg, Maja and Riley watched as Mum and Florence caught up on the last thirteen years. Riley saw her mother crumple up when she found out her own father was dead. She saw Florence reach over to comfort her. They cried and apologised and, best of all, forgave each other.

Riley watched Mum being cradled by Florence. She'd never thought about her mum being a daughter.

But she was. She was somebody's child. Mum needed to be looked after by her own mother now.

Florence kissed her daughter's cheeks and wiped the tears from her eyes, just like Alison did to Riley, and Riley felt a huge weight being lifted off her shoulders. She didn't have to look after her mum on her own. Florence would help.

Maybe, just maybe, Riley could go back to being a regular kid again.

CHAPTER 25

ONE MONTH LATER ...

Riley came downstairs to the smell of bacon. She opened the kitchen door and saw Mum and Florence side by side at the cooker, making breakfast.

'Ouch,' Mum said.

'What happened?' Florence looked concerned.

'It's nothing – I just burnt the tip of my finger.'

'Here, let me see.' Florence examined Mum's finger and then held it under some cold running water.

Riley smiled. It was lovely to see Mum being looked after and fussed over. In the last month Florence had built Mum's health right back up. She had made sure she rested, and ate properly, and took all her medicine and tons of vitamins and supplements too. Mum looked so well now, healthy and happy. The worry had gone from her face.

Florence's house was big and clean, and Riley had her own bedroom with a double bed and a proper wardrobe. She shared a big bathroom with Mum. Each day, when she had a shower, she closed her eyes and enjoyed every second of the hot water running down her body.

The first week they'd spent in Florence's house, Riley had just slept and slept. Florence said it was her mind finally allowing her body to rest.

'You've been on high alert,' she had explained, 'worrying about everything. That is very draining. Now you need to let both your body and mind rest. It's really important that you sleep.' Florence had tucked Riley in and left a glass of water beside her bed. She'd kissed her on the forehead. 'I know we have only known each other for a short while, but I am so proud of you, Riley. You are an exceptional girl. But now, I want you to let me look after you. It's time for you to be a child again. You've had to be an adult for too long. Close your eyes and have sweet, happy dreams.'

Riley had done exactly that. For the past month her nightmares had stopped and she now had nice dreams or no dreams at all. She felt happy again. Her feelings of stress and her headaches were gone. Her constant exhaustion was gone. She felt like a kid again.

Mum looked up and saw Riley standing at the kitchen door. 'Hello, sweetie, did you sleep well?'

'Brilliantly.' Riley grinned.

Alison came over and hugged her. 'Good. Breakfast is ready.'

The three women sat down and ate together. It felt so normal. Riley had thought it would be weird, but it was the opposite: it felt like home.

Florence poured Alison a cup of tea and put the teapot down. 'Riley, we need to talk to you about something,' she said.

Uh oh. What now? Riley frowned.

Mum took Riley's hand in hers. 'I know there has been a lot of change in your life. But Mum has asked us to stay here in Rockstone, with her. It would mean a new school and a new life. If you don't want to, that's fine. We'll work something out. It's your decision, Riley. Whatever you want, we'll do.'

Riley sat back in her chair. Did she want to move here forever? Leave Dublin? Her life? Her school? Her friends?

But what life did she have? Things since Dad had died had been worse every day, and the last few months had been hell. She had no home there. Her school friends? The only friend she'd really miss was Sophie, and even though she loved Sophie, would her friend ever truly be able to understand what Riley had been through? Riley was different now. This whole experience had changed her. She felt she had very little in common with her old friends. And, if she was being honest, it would be a relief to get away from Vanessa and her poisonous personality.

The people she'd really miss were Maja and Oleg. They had been her rocks through all of this. They had been her true friends, the people who had helped her survive.

A new school and a new life. It sounded good to Riley. She could start all over again. The new Riley, in a new school. She'd make new friends. No more lying, no more stealing, no more shame, no more anxiety. A brand-new life. A new start for her and Mum.

Her mum would be able to be a mum again. Her granny would look after them and they'd never have to live in a car again.

'Yes,' Riley said. 'I'd like to move here. My answer is yes.'

Mum went over and hugged her. Florence wiped tears from her eyes. *This is what happy feels like,* Riley thought. *This is family. This is love. This is what life is about: love and kindness.*

CHAPTER 26

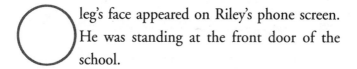leg's face appeared on Riley's phone screen. He was standing at the front door of the school.

'Hi, Riley, I'm here with Maja, we're waiting for Sophie.'

Maja's face appeared on the screen. 'Hi, Riley.'

Riley smiled and waved at her two friends. 'Hi from Galway. Thanks so much for doing this for me.'

'I'm going to take you off FaceTime now and put you on speaker so you can listen in discreetly.' Oleg's face disappeared.

Riley went back to biting her thumbnail nervously.

'Maybe we missed her?' Maja said.

'I know what she looks like – we haven't missed her,' Oleg replied.

'Maybe your eyes are not so good.'

'My eyes are fine,' Oleg replied. 'Stop distracting me or I *will* miss her.'

'I say nothing, you are the one talking now,' Maja noted.

Riley giggled. Those two never stopped bickering. 'How is the restaurant, Maja?' she asked.

'It's good, but we miss you and Alison.'

'We miss you too – and your food! How is school, Oleg?'

'Same as usual, Riley, but very soon I will be home hugging my children.'

'I'm so glad for you,' Riley said.

'I want Oleg to come work for me,' Maja said.

Oleg laughed. 'Maja, if I worked for you we'd kill each other. I could never have you as my boss.'

'I am not so bad,' Maja said. 'I am good boss. Riley, am I good boss?'

'Yes, you are, Maja. But I think Oleg is right. You'd probably kill each other.'

Maja laughed. 'Maybe this is true. Oleg is not doing what I tell him.'

'Exactly!' Oleg laughed. 'Wait, there she is. Sophie?' he called out.

Riley heard Sophie's voice. 'Yes?'

Vanessa's voice was unmistakable. 'What do you want? How do you know her name?'

'Who are you?' Maja asked.

'Who are *you*? Do you even work here?' Vanessa demanded.

'Oh, I know you, you are the nasty girl I hear about. Nasty snake girl. *Sssssssssss,*' Maja hissed.

Riley put her hand over her mouth so she wouldn't laugh out loud. She didn't want Sophie or Vanessa to know she could hear them.

'Oh my God, I'm reporting you. How dare you speak to me like that?!'

'Maybe I will report you if you don't shut up,' Maja snapped.

'Sophie,' Oleg said calmly, 'this is a letter from Riley

to you. She very specifically asked that you read it in private,' he added firmly.

'Oh, OK, thanks, I will,' Sophie said.

'Open it now,' Vanessa said.

'Hey, snake girl, are you deaf also? He said private, OK?' Maja said.

'I'm going to get you fired, whoever you are.'

Maja whooped. 'Snake girl is stupid too. I am not working here. But be careful, snake girl – if you put out poison, poison comes back to you.'

'Sophie! Like, hello, could you defend me, please?'

'You were rude, Vanessa, and it's your problem, not mine. Thank you for the letter. I will read it in private.'

Yes, Riley thought. Sophie was finally standing up to Vanessa.

'Do you have Riley's new number?' Sophie asked.

'No,' Oleg lied. Riley wasn't ready to talk to anyone. She wanted peace and quiet. Time to adjust to her new life. She wanted to live in the bubble of just her mum and her granny for a bit. She wanted to savour the security and safety and love that now surrounded her.

She'd call Sophie in a while, when she was fully settled into her new life.

'Well, if you're talking to her, please tell her I miss her and I hope she's OK.'

'Why do you even care?' Vanessa asked. 'Riley was weird and a liar.'

'No, she wasn't.' Sophie raised her voice. 'She was my best friend, and she was kind and nice and thoughtful. I think she was having a really hard time and I don't think I was there for her enough. So shut up and go away, Vanessa, you are the most annoying person in the world. If you weren't my cousin, I wouldn't even talk to you.'

Go Sophie! Riley cheered silently.

'They've gone,' Oleg whispered into the phone after a minute.

'Snake girl is chasing after cousin, but Sophie is running away.' Maja laughed.

'Thanks for doing that for me,' Riley said.

'Oleg could do it by himself but I want to see Sophie and snake cousin. I think Sophie is nice but weak. She needs to be stronger. Snake girl will always be snake. You make nice new friends in Galway, no snakes. OK?'

'Yes, I will.'

'OK, I have to go now. Talk soon.'

'Bye, Maja, and thank you.'

'I'd better get to work too,' Oleg said. 'You take good care, Riley. I'm here for you if you need anything.'

'Bye, Oleg, talk soon and thank you, thank you for all your kindness.'

'It was my pleasure.'

He hung up, and Riley felt like the luckiest girl in the world to have two such amazing people on her side.

Dear Sophie,

I'm really sorry for disappearing and not filling you in on what has been going on. My life has been a bit of a nightmare recently, but I was too ashamed to tell you about how bad it was.

Dad lost all his money, and we got kicked out of our house and ended up living in our car. It was really scary and then Mum got sick.

Oleg, the caretaker at school, and Maja, the woman who owns the restaurant Mum was washing dishes in, helped to keep us alive. Without their kindness, I don't think we would have survived.

I know you'll say I should have told you, and you and your family would have helped us, but I didn't want anyone to know. I was so embarrassed and stressed about it all.

In the end, I went and found my granny, my mum's mum. They hadn't spoken in years, but they've made up and she has taken us in and been amazing. I live in Galway with her now and Mum is better and life is good again.

We're going to stay here. Mum's going back to college and I'm starting a new school in September. I want you to know that you are a great friend and I will really miss you.

The reason there is a ten euro note in the envelope is because I took a tube of Pringles and a packet of chocolate fingers from your house when I was starving and I'm so ashamed. Your mum was always so nice to me. Please explain to her and tell her I'm so sorry. I'm sorry you got into trouble for it too. I will never do anything like that again.

What I've learned from this whole experience is that you never know what is going on in someone else's life and that small acts of kindness can make a huge difference.

I've also realised that friends come in all forms, some your own age, but also adults and people from all over the world. In fact, it's the people who have suffered themselves who seem more likely to notice when someone else is in trouble.

I hope that I will be able to help someone in trouble myself one day. When everything is taken away from you, you realise that the only things that really matter are kindness and love.

I'll call you when things are more settled here and maybe your mum would let you come and visit some time? I'd love to see you and explain everything face to face.

I miss you,

Riley xx

A few days later, Riley got a reply:

Dear Riley

I cried so much when I read your letter that I literally have no tears left in my body. I had NO idea you were going through so much. I wish that you had told me. I would have helped you – you *could have lived with us! But I understand you were embarrassed and didn't want to tell anyone.*

You should never be embarrassed with me, though, Riley. I'm your best friend. I'd never judge you. I knew things were hard for you – you were so quiet and you seemed so worried all the time. I wish now that I had asked more questions, but when I did ask, you always seemed to change the subject, so I didn't think you wanted to talk about it. I'm sorry I was such a bad friend. I should have tried harder to find out why you were so sad. I guess I thought it was because of your dad. I feel terrible about letting you down.

Mum said under NO circumstances will she accept the ten euros from you and that you are the bravest and most amazing girl in the world. She says you are to come and stay any time you want for as long as you want, and she will fill the whole house with chocolate fingers and Pringles for you.

I really miss you. Vanessa is such a cow, I'm sick of her. She is so mean about everyone. I'm so glad the summer holidays are almost here. I'm going to stay as far away from her as possible. Mum has asked the headmistress of the secondary school to put us in different classes next year, thank God.

I can't believe you won't be back next year, and I will miss you so much – but I'm really happy that you found your grandmother and that she is looking after you and your mum. I am blown away by how strong you've been. You're amazing, Riley. I'm so sorry I wasn't a better friend. I have learned a lot from this. Mum says we need to be more aware of other people and their problems, and we've signed up to help at a soup kitchen every Sunday.

The older boys are going to boarding school in September, but Mum said she couldn't let go of the twins just yet. So the house will be 50 per cent less noisy at least.

Anyway, I love you, I miss you, and I am so sorry that I wasn't a better friend. I hope that you have the most AMAZING life in Galway and make loads of new friends – but don't forget me. Mum said I can visit you as soon as you're ready for visitors.

Your bestie,

Sophie x

P.S. You're right that the most important things are love and kindness. I'm going to try to be better at both. Even with my annoying brothers … ☺ ☺ ☺

Riley folded up the letter and tucked it under her pillow to read again later. She was glad she had told Sophie the truth at last – the truth about Riley. She lay back on her soft bed and cuddled Tiger. Life was only going to get better from now on. She just knew it.

Acknowledgements

A book is written by the author, but behind the scenes, many people help to make it better and get it out into the world.

A big thank you to:

My skilled editor, Venetia Gosling.

Dedicated publicist, Fiona Murphy.

My fantastic agent, Marianne Gunn O'Connor.

Brilliant copyeditor, Esther Ní Dhonnacha.

All the team at Gill Books who have been so fantastic to work with and who are so passionate about getting books out into the world.

My three children, Hugo, Geordy and Amy, who all read this book and told me which 'boring bits' to take out and which 'good bits' to leave in.

Troy for supporting me and cheering me on all the way.

My mum, my sister and my brother. I was lucky enough to grow up in a lovely home full of books and learned to love reading from an early age.

My friends who were on Zoom all through Covid, making the long days in lockdown shorter.

My two cats, Minnie and Luna, who come to purr (or grunt – Minnie can't purr, she grunts) on my lap when I'm writing.

Peter McVerry, who, along with all of his volunteers, does such life-changing work for homeless people. And to all the people working with the homeless and providing services for them to help keep them safe.

Most of all, I want to thank you, my readers. I love writing stories and I hope you enjoy reading them too. Reading a book is the best way to disappear from life for a while. Never stop reading – it's the best way to escape reality!

Further Information

n this book, Riley and her mum become homeless and have to live in the boot of their car. Sadly, this is not as unusual as you might think. Homelessness is an issue experienced by people who lack a place to live that is supportive, affordable, decent and secure. As of February 2022, over ten thousand people were accessing emergency accommodation in Ireland. Almost three thousand of these people are children. These figures do not include people sleeping on the streets, people sleeping on couches in their friends' houses waiting to find a place to live, homeless people in hospitals and prisons, and those in direct provision centres.

If you want to know more about homelessness and how to help, you can visit the Peter McVerry Trust website: https://pmvtrust.ie/